HUNTING FOR LOVE

A COLLECTION OF HUNTERS BOOK TWO

TOBY WISE

Hunting for Love© 2022 by Toby Wise

All rights reserved. No part of this book may be used or reproduced in any manner whatsoever without written permission except in the case of brief quotations for book reviews.

This book is a work of fiction. Names, characters, businesses, organizations, places, events, and incidents either are the product of the author's imagination or are used fictitiously. Any resemblance to actual persons, living or dead, events, or locales is entirely coincidental.

Book cover by Vicki Brostenianc

Beta Services by Kirk from LesCourt

Proofreading by Alee

Formatting by Pumpkin Author Services

PROLOGUE
ZANDER

Fear leaves me breathless.

Pain lances through my leg and a yelp leaves my throat. Fuck. Fuck, this can't be happening. This cannot be real. I grit my teeth, doing my best not to look as panicked as I feel. I look over at my son, JJ. "Look away, baby."

JJ begins to sniffle and I do my best to shake off the pain. I'm okay. This is okay. We'll get out of this. I need to calm him down. I don't want him to be scared or worried.

"Are you okay, Papa?"

"I'm okay, sweetie. Just give me a second to figure out how to get my foot free, okay?" He nods his head, still keeping his back to me. Without his eyes on me, I take a moment to assess just how bad this is.

Fuck.

My foot is caught in a fucking hunting trap. How the hell did this happen? I thought we were basically home free! I thought we'd be okay. The only thing not sending me into a full blown panic is knowing that we're not too far from the road.

"I'm gonna try to get myself out of the trap. Just keep looking over there, okay?"

"Okay," JJ says, his voice wavers and I know I have to move fast before he gets curious and looks. I don't want him to see all this blood.

I sit down in the grass as carefully as I can before reaching down and trying to pull the trap open. I'm not sure how these things even work and no matter how much I try I can't seem to pry it open. Fuck. Panic is setting in and I do everything I can to breathe through it, to push it away. I need to think. How can I get out of this?

"Okay, baby, change of plans," I say carefully. I reach over and put my hands on JJ's shoulders. "I need you to shift. Can you do that for me?"

"I can do that," he says softly.

"I know you can. After you shift, I'm gonna shift too. And then we're gonna run over towards the road, okay? I need you to stay *right* next to me and not shift until I do. Do you understand?"

"I understand," JJ says. I hear him take a deep breath and between one blink and another, he begins to shift into his shifter skin.

I have to be quick. I'm hoping that I can move as I shift. With my cat paw being so small, just maybe I'll be able to tug my paw free from the trap.

I look inward, finding the connection I share with my inner animal. Once I'm ready, I shift. As the shift washes over me, I pull my paw away from the trap and thankfully, I'm able to get my paw completely free. Relief floods me so hard I just barely keep myself from tipping over and laying in the grass. The pain lancing through me keeps me steady though.

JJ meows at me, the sound questioning. I nudge his face with my head, rubbing myself against him to help soothe his worry. My scent rubs off on him and his onto me, helping keep us both grounded. We're okay. We'll be okay.

I begin trekking towards the road, making sure JJ is beside me as we go. If we were real cats, JJ would probably be bigger than me by now but because we're shifters, his cat form is much smaller. JJ hates it when I pick him up by the scruff of his neck and carry him around. He says he's too old for that, but I still reserve the right to use that method in case of emergencies.

Emerging onto the pavement makes me breathe easy for the first time since I realized my foot was stuck in that stupid trap. I look both ways, wondering where to go from here.

My ears pick up footsteps and I make a noise, letting JJ know to freeze. We slowly step back until we're mostly hidden in the grass by the sidewalk. I wait, listening, making sure it's not someone we know.

I take a deep breath and my entire body locks up. A meow leaves my lips without my permission.

That scent. It's like nothing I've ever smelled before. It smells so good and my inner omega instantly craves it, demanding we find the source of it so we can smell it up close and personal. I keep my feet planted, gritting my teeth as I fight my instincts.

My eyes catch a figure walking down the street, his hands in his pockets. It's no one I've ever seen before and the last of the tension making my chest tight seems to loosen. This isn't John. We're safe.

I take a tentative step forward. JJ stays glued to my side. I take another step, a pained meow leaving my throat without my permission as I put weight on my hurt paw. Fuck. How could I forget that I was hurt? Just because I'm smelling the most amazing scent I've ever experienced in my life doesn't mean I've lost all of my common sense.

"Hello?"

JJ meows, a nervous sound that makes my heart clench. The man on the sidewalk freezes as his eyes find us. He's a complete stranger and yet, there's a weird feeling in my stomach, whispering that I can trust him.

"Oh dear," the man whispers, getting on his knees near us. He holds out his hand. "Are you hurt? Come here. I'll take care of you. Poor things."

JJ looks at me and I give him a tiny nod. JJ steps forward and the man carefully runs the back of his fingers over JJ's head. JJ leans into the touch. I meow and the man smiles, the sight making *something* go through my stomach.

The man takes off his hoodie before reaching out slowly, making sure I won't bite him before scooping me up into his arms. He cradles me against his chest with such care. Then he reaches down and picks up JJ. JJ buries his face against me and I can tell he's just as relieved as I am.

I feel safe. I feel like JJ is safe. My body goes slack in this random stranger's arms.

Being tucked into this man's sweater makes something crystal clear. It would seem Lady Fate has a bit of an ironic sense of humor. I've somehow run away from my litter straight into the arms of my true mate.

CHAPTER ONE
RONNY

I HOLD the precious cargo in my arms as gently as possible, happy that these cats aren't squirming or trying to jump out of my arms. As soon as I'd seen the two of them, I knew I had to do something. One of them was just a baby and the other had a terrible limp. As I look down, I notice their leg is bloody.

"You poor thing," I murmur softly, holding them in one arm and using my free hand to pet their head. "Don't worry. I promise I'll take care of you."

As I carry them upstairs into Axel's apartment, I can't help but wonder if I should be calling a local vet or animal shelter. But the idea of giving these cats to someone instead of taking care of them myself fills my stomach with dread. I can't do that. It has to be me.

Being a hunter, I know a thing or two about basic first aid. I'm sure I can take care of this leg myself. I'm not *only* good with computers. Though if I'm honest, I'm not mad that I'm usually left in my camper instead of heading into the thick of hunts.

Our group's leader, Jeff, was recently turned into a vampire. He's come through the transformation with grace and more self-control I didn't even realize he possessed, and on top of that, he also has a vampire mate named Axel.

Mates are kind of a weird concept for me since I'm human through and through, but I can see the way these two have fallen for each other. Hell, Jeff was willing to do anything to protect Axel. A tiny part of my chest longs for something like that, a love so firm it transcends all understanding. But being a human means that's probably not something I'll ever experience. But a boy can dream.

My finger slides over the cat's head over and over until I'm not sure if it's more soothing for them or me. They lean into my touch which in turn, makes me smile.

I step into Axel's apartment, finding the living room completely deserted. There's a woman here, Star, smiling at me like she was waiting for me. She's a midwife who came to help Axel and Jeff bring their baby into the world. She feels *special* to me somehow but I can't really put my finger on it. Call it hunter intuition but I would be shocked if she was actually human.

I give her a smile, feeling a little out of place with her here. She deserves my respect, more so than a stranger. Not that that makes a lick of sense, but here we are.

"Found something outside, dear?"

I nod my head. "A couple of strays."

"You're not the only person I know who collects strays," she says with a wide smile. "And in their case, it worked out quite splendidly. I have a feeling this time will be no different."

"Umm," I murmur, not really knowing what I'm supposed to say to that. "Thank you?"

"You're welcome. And when the time is right, I'll find you again," she adds with a tiny wink before going into the bedroom. I follow behind, wanting to meet Jeff and Axel's new baby. At least, that's what I assume is happening in the bedroom.

"Ronny!" Martin greets, "Come meet Lily!"

I look around at my team, all gathered around the bed to meet our newest crewmate when the tiniest meow comes from the hoodie in my arms. I feel my face flush as all eyes point towards me.

"I umm, I might have found some new friends," I say sheepishly, just barely keeping myself from rubbing at the back of my neck, knowing that could lead to me dropping my precious bundle and that's the *last* thing I wanna do right now.

Carlos, the youngest of our hunting crew, steps over to me and I take a step back out of instinct. I'm not sure what the heck is going on with me right now. I know Carlos would *never* hurt an animal but everything inside of me is screaming for me to protect these cats, even from him. "Sorry," he says gently. "Just wanted to see."

"That's okay. Just be careful, they're hurt," I say, wanting him to understand. When Carlos nods, I gently pull back my hoodie, letting him see the cats.

Carlos' body goes tense before he's murmuring, "Ronny, they're--"

I cut him off. "Hurt. I know. I found them outside and I couldn't just let them go. So I grabbed them. I'll take good care of them." I look down at the cats, a small smile forming across my lips. I gently touch the adult cat who meows at me in response.

"Are you sure you wanna take them on the road with us, Ronny? I heard you found us a new job," Jeff says from his place on the bed beside Axel.

I nod my head, my brows furrowing. The idea of leaving these cats here makes me sick to my stomach. I can't leave them, I just can't. "I can take care of them, no worries, bossman."

Speaking of the job, I think back to the research that I've been doing. There's been some stories online about a wishing well that truly grants people's wishes. Which is all well and fun until someone wishes that someone's dead, or wishes that someone gets sick and it actually comes true. This will be a quick job by my calculations. We can find the well and put it through a cleansing ritual to destroy the magic being used to make these wishes come true. In and out as long as nothing complicates things.

In my experience, there's a solid fifty fifty chance of things being more complicated than they seem so we'll do our best to be prepared for anything.

I'll have to get Cooper on research as soon as possible. Cooper is our lore guy. He has books upon books upon books in his library. He's constantly adding to his collection with every single city we visit. He's not only book smart, but also fit to be out in the action if needs be.

If there's anything that could bring a wishing well to life, Cooper would be able to find it.

The newly made parents look down lovingly at their baby and something like longing hits me in the chest. I've never really been someone to dream about a partner and kids, but seeing how happy they are sparks something inside me. Maybe I would be a better dad than my own. Maybe I'd fall into the same supernatural trap that he did.

I shake my head, looking down at the cats tucked in my arms. The little one lets out a little snore as he sleeps while the adult cat stares up at me with wide, green eyes. I sneak out through the same door I'd come into, quickly finding Axel's bathroom.

"Okay," I whisper, looking through his cabinets and finding some cleaning supplies and some bandages. It seems Axel, despite being a vampire, had everything he might have needed to help someone in need. That's perfect because right now, that's exactly what I need to help my little furry friends.

I lay them both in the sink, making sure my hoodie cushions them nicely before getting to work cleaning up the wounds on the adult cat. I'm careful as I move, doing my best to make this as painless as possible. The poor thing has been hurt enough, I don't need to accidentally add to that.

"There we go," I whisper, using the bandages and wrapping them around the cat's paw. "All better for now. We'll check it in a few days and clean it as needed." I feel silly talking to the cat but I can't stop myself from doing it, hoping they'll somehow understand my intent. "We're gonna be loading you up into my RV for a road trip. I hope that's alright."

Those giant green eyes meet mine and I *swear* they give me a nod in understanding. I tilt my head to the side and they copy the gesture. Huh. Weird.

Before I can think more about it, Martin is knocking on the door to check on me. After assuring him that everything is alright, the four of us, Martin, Carlos, Cooper, and myself, head back to our RVs for the night to give the new parents some privacy with Lily.

CHAPTER TWO
ZANDER

I watch as the human who found us places us gently on his bed. I heard his friend call him *Ronny*. My true mate's name is Ronny. I'm still having a hard time wrapping my head around this whole situation.

He's brought us to an RV, which is a strange way to live. Though, I can't really judge, thinking back to what I've just escaped from. This is a vast improvement.

JJ stretches out beside me, letting out the most adorable yawn. More and more I'm glad I finally made that decision to get the fuck out.

I take in a deep breath, getting hit full force with Ronny's scent while we're laying in his bed. Fuck. It's the most perfect scent that I've ever experienced. It's lemony and bright and all things good in the world. I take a step out of his hoodie just so I can bury my face in his sheets, rubbing myself against his scent to let it wash all over me. I should be embarrassed but there's something about being in this form that lets my inhibitions be more carefree.

"

Ronny thinks I'm a cat and a cat would rub themselves against these soft sheets.

"Make yourself at home," he says with a wide smile, rubbing the top of my head. I lean into his touch, wishing I could shift into my human form and hug him tight. But I stop myself from thinking about that too hard.

Ronny's a *human*. Sure, he seems to be friends with some vampires and that guy who smells like a wet dog who I'm *pretty* sure is a type of canine shifter, but that doesn't mean he's okay with other supernatural creatures. It doesn't mean he won't freak out when he finds out the cat he's been taking care of is actually a man.

I'll wait just a little while longer. Ronny mentioned taking a drive to a new location. Plus, my paw needs to finish healing. I'll just wait until I'm feeling better and then I'll shift. It'll be fine.

That'll give me time to sit and see what kind of people these guys are. It'll give me time to see what kind of person *Ronny* is.

My eyes widen as Ronny pulls off his shirt. Oh my gods. I greedily take him in. He's lean but strong with the smallest spattering of chest hair in the center of his chest. There's a fine line of hair that leads from his belly button down into his jeans. His eyes are a rich, dark color that matches his dark hair. My stomach squirms in the most pleasant way at the sight. My true mate is *hot*.

The thought stops me in my tracks. My true mate. I can't believe I've found my *true mate*.

John used to say so many things to keep me under his thumb. One of them was that *he* was my true mate and that to leave him would be going against Lady Fate herself. Now that I've found Ronny, I can't help but feel even more bitter towards John. He was never my true mate. He never smelled like home the way this man does. Gods, I wish I could go back and get the years back that John stole from me but I can't, all I can do is live the best life now that I have freedom.

I'm allowed to make choices now. I'm allowed to decide what's best for me and JJ without someone breathing down my neck telling me I can't trust myself.

I decide to stay right where I am. This feels right. I might not be able to rely on Ronny. For all I know he's a mass murderer who's taking us across the country to find his next victim. But now I have the ability to run away if push comes to shove. I'm not *stuck*. And now that I'm more attuned with my instincts, I trust that Lady Fate wouldn't push me from one douche to another. Ronny feels different.

Ronny starts to hum a soft song as he throws on some sweatpants and a hoodie. My eyes follow him as he steps out of his bedroom. In this form, I'm allowed to stare from my place on the bed as he sits down at a computer, his fingers flying faster than I thought possible across the keys. I lay my head on JJ's, snuggling close and letting his warmth sink into my skin. I lick his ear, letting him know I'm here and that we're safe. He nuzzles me right back.

JJ is the one good thing that John gave me. I'm thankful for my little boy every single day that we're both alive. We're free.

As my eyes grow heavy, soothed by the sound of Ronny typing on his keyboard, I can't help but think about the future. Now that I'm away from John, the future is a mass space of opportunity. I could quite literally do anything. It's overwhelming. It's exhilarating. But my mind continues to drift back to Ronny and this crew. They all seem so *good* at first glance. I hope I'm not wrong about them.

And Ronny. Handsome, caring Ronny who found a hurt cat and immediately picked them up, promising to take care of them. I want his gentle hands on me again, running through my hair. I want those full lips against my own. I want him to form a relationship with JJ. Oh gods, I hate how drawn I am already, but that's having true mate I suppose. A supernatural tug towards that person.

Hopefully Ronny will be okay that I have a kid. Gods, what am I even thinking? Can I really tell this human that I'm his true mate? Would he even *want* a true mate? Is he even attracted to other men?

Instead of letting all these worries wash me away, I shake them away. I can worry about them tomorrow. For now, I'm going to rest and regain my strength. I'm going to trust that this is truly the hand of Lady Fate, guiding me to where I'm supposed to be. I close my eyes and for the first time in *years*, I sleep without a shadow of doom hovering over me. I sleep peacefully.

CHAPTER THREE
RONNY

THE TREES all blur together as I cruise down the highway in my RV. My head bobs up and down in tune with the song playing on the radio. I can't stop thinking about our case. It's not every day that we find a case involving such strong magic.

Cooper has a few theories. One of possibilities is the well being cursed by someone after their wish didn't come true. Another theory is that there's someone living in the well, granting these wishes and purposely causing chaos just for the fun of it. I really, really hope it's not the second one. Magic, we can easily deal with. Talking someone out of doing shitty things? That's usually a lot harder.

It makes me think back to my father. When one sells their soul for enough money to pay off their gambling debt, things don't always go exactly as planned.

Before I can go fully down that road, there's a tiny meow to my right. I look over, only slightly startled by the little gray cat looking up at me. I smile down at them. "Hey there, little buddy," I murmur, holding out my hand. They run their face against my hand and that's all the permission I need to tug them up and set them on my lap.

With one hand on the steering wheel and the other petting this little cat, I continue to drive. I wish I knew where these cuties came from. Is someone out there looking for their loved pets? I'm not sure why but I truly don't think so. There's something about them that just resonates deep within my chest. They belong here with me.

I can't explain it. But then again, there's so much in my line of work that simply cannot be explained. Like Jeff being turned into a vampire, or the idea of two vampires being able to have a baby together. Or magic in general. It's so far out of my wheelhouse that I simply accept it and move on to my computer where I can find numbers and stats and algorithms. Those things I get. That's how I can help this team.

My thumb runs over the kitten's head between their ears over and over until they're tucked into my lap letting out the tiniest little snores. It makes me happy, knowing they trust me enough to sleep like this.

Another meow catches my attention. Oh no. The sound doesn't sound pleased. It sounds panicked and worried.

"It's okay," I call out, ignoring the way I know they can't understand me. "They're up here with me. Your baby is safe."

I hear little footsteps run through my RV towards the front and a moment later, the adult cat is jumping into the passenger seat. They stare at me for a long time, almost like they're assessing me. I must pass their judgment because they sit in the passenger seat without a fight for their baby.

"Everything's okay," I tell them seriously, "you're safe with me. I promise."

Those giant green eyes blink at me before the cat is laying down, their head against their paws, but their eyes continue to watch me. It's almost like they wanna make sure I mean what I say. I don't plan to prove my words wrong. Even to a cat.

Before I can stop myself, I start talking to the cat, just to pass the time while driving.

"I'm not from around here," I tell them, keeping an eye on the RV in front of me, following Jeff's lead. "I'm from a tiny town in the middle of nowhere. The type of place where everyone knows your business and you know all of theirs. Real unfortunate when your old man is a mean son of a bitch that was so grouchy no one wanted to be around him."

I look over and the cat blinks at me, seeming to be hanging on my every word. I give them a little shrug. "I don't have to deal with him anymore. He's long gone and when he died, I finally got myself out of that little hell hole of a place. Sure, some might see that as running away but honestly, sometimes that's the best thing you can do for yourself. You know what I mean?"

The cat seems to give me a barely there nod, his eyes blinking slowly at me. That makes me smile. I'm pretty sure I read somewhere that cats blink slowly at people they love or trust. Maybe I'm gaining their trust.

"I've always been really good at computers," I tell the

cat because really, why am I bringing up my sob story of a past? The cat doesn't wanna hear about the day I killed my first monster. No one needs to hear about that. There's a reason all five of us became hunters and it's not because of the amazing benefits package. "They're really fun and interesting and you can find just about anything on the internet. I developed a software that essentially combs through local newspapers across the country, compiling data that helps us find our next case. I'm always tweaking it to make it better. That's how I found this case, actually."

At that, the cat meows, tilting their head to the side. Before I can explain what a case is, I notice Jeff turning off the highway. Must be bathroom break time.

"We're about to stop for a bathroom break," I tell them, turning on my turn signal. "Maybe you'd like to jump outside and stretch your legs. I just realized I probably should have gotten you a litter box or something so you don't have to wait for us to pull over. Hmm."

The cat meows again, standing up and putting their front paws on the dash to look out the windshield. Oh my gods, they're absolutely adorable. I wish I knew more about them. Like if they're domestic or if they're wild. Why were they wandering out in the woods and what happened to their paw? My fingers pet the baby's ears as I drive, my curiosity getting the best of me. I decide I'll check online and make sure there's not a missing cat ad anywhere.

Every part of my being wants to keep these cats here with me but I'd never steal someone's beloved pet.

We pull into a rest stop, parking our RV's at a distance from the shelter, not wanting to get in the way of people's regular sized cars. I stretch my arms over my head, a satisfying pop coming from my spine.

"Ready to stretch your legs?"

I get a resounding meow in response and I smile so wide my cheeks hurt. After waking the baby cat up, I open the RV and watch them bound outside, realizing with a start there's a chance they won't come back.

Just as the thought passes my head, the adult cat looks back at me, blinking slowly. They'll come back. I just know it.

CHAPTER FOUR
ZANDER

I LEAP ONTO THE FLOOR, bumping my head with JJ's as Ronny opens the RV doors. We step out into the sun, stretching as we go. It feels nice to be outside, but at the same time, being in Ronny's RV feels homey and safe.

JJ lets out the cutest meow, jumping on me and wrestling me to the ground. I could easily tackle him back and pin him to the ground, but I keep playing with him, letting him get the pent up energy from being stuck in an RV out.

Once JJ starts to peter out, I push him away with my paw. He lets out a giant yawn, finding a nice spot at the back of the RV to lay in the grass. He finds the perfect sunbeam and my chest warms at the sight.

The guys are all chatting together and one of the vampires comes out, holding his baby against his chest. He looks so *happy*. More and more I feel like I've stumbled upon just what I need.

"You know we're hunters, right?"

I startle, jumping to my feet and staring up at the guy I've heard people call Carlos. I completely freeze as he gazes down at me. He squats down so he's even closer and I just barely stay standing where I am instead of running away.

"We're not gonna hurt you. But I thought you'd like to know."

Everything in me is screaming to grab JJ and run away. John used to tell me how evil hunters were. How they would hunt me down if I ever thought about running away. He told me he had hunter friends who would find me no matter how far away I ran so it was always better just to stay where I was.

Would Lady Fate truly see me escape one evil man only for my true mate to be a different brand of evil?

I don't think she would do that.

I look up at Carlos and tilt my head. I take a deep breath and realize the reason he knows I'm a shifter is because he's one himself. Some sort of canine but nothing I've ever smelled before. That fills me with a little bit of hope. If these hunters allow a shifter to hunt alongside them, maybe they'd be okay with JJ and I.

"We're not gonna hurt you. We're good. You're not gonna screw us over, are you? I just have to ask because I'm rather protective of these guys and you've seemed to worm your way into Ronny's heart already."

I shake my head, needing him to know that I would never hurt Ronny. There's no way for me to speak in this form but I hope Carlos will understand. He nods his head and I feel my body relax.

"Can you shift into your human form?"

I shake my head, holding up my paw. It's better if I let it completely heal before shifting. I might be able to heal supernaturally fast compared to humans but that trap really did a number on my foot.

"Alright. Let's go find your kiddo. I think I saw him run after Ronny towards the bathrooms," Carlos says and my head raises. Fuck. How did I not notice JJ running away? I try my best to let my anxiety fade away into the background as I walk with Carlos towards the bathrooms. What John told me was a lie. These people aren't going to hurt me or JJ. These hunters keep company with another shifter and two vampires, of course they're not just hunting supernatural beings for being different. Everything is okay.

"Ronny?"

Terror fills my stomach for the second time in such a short period. Instead of freezing, I leap into action, putting myself between JJ and Ronny.

Instead of a small kitten in the grass, I find my son standing at his full human height wearing Ronny's hoodie which covers him down to his shins. Oh gods. Why has he shifted?

I look up at Ronny, finding him staring at me, his eyes flicking between me and JJ. Carlos steps up beside Ronny, putting his hand on Ronny's shoulder. The tiniest growl sounds through my chest before I can stop it.

"Hey," Carlos murmurs, his voice gentle and calming. "What's going on here?"

"I'm--" Ronny finally tears his eyes away to look at

Carlos. "I'm really confused. My kitten just turned into a little boy."

"Yeah. Shifters do that sometimes," Carlos says with an amused smile.

I stand my ground, my eyes never leaving Ronny. Is this it? Is this the moment he rejects me and my son? Will this be too much for him to handle? The thought of Ronny rejecting me leaves me breathless but I'm strong, I can take it. If I can run away from John I can handle *anything* life throws at me.

"Shifters?" Ronny finally looks down at me. "Are you a shifter?" I nod my head, letting out a little meow. His face brightens with a blush. "Oh gods. That's so embarrassing! I was chatting to you so much while I was driving because I thought you were just a cat!"

Carlos chuckles and I finally feel like I can breathe again. He's not upset with me. I let out a mournful meow, my own way of apologizing. Somehow, Ronny knows exactly what I mean.

"It's okay," he tells me, squatting down and holding out his hand. I lean close, brushing my cheek against it. "It's not your fault. I'm not upset. The plan is still the same, I want to help you get better."

A pitiful meow leaves my lips without my permission. I can't believe he still wants to help me, he wants to keep me. My brain whispers *for now*, but I do my best to ignore that. Little hands reach down and pick me up. I dangle with his arms under my armpits. Gods, this is incredibly undignified. This must be payback for all the times I picked him up by the back of his neck.

"This is my Papa," JJ tells Ronny and Carlos. "He hurt his paw so we had to shift. He told me I was supposed to stay in my cat form but I really had to use the bathroom so I thought it would be okay."

"It's okay," Carlos tells him. "You and your Papa are safe with us. You don't have to be afraid."

"I'm not afraid of anything," JJ says, puffing out his chest. My little alpha is fearless.

"I'm sure you're not, kiddo," Ronny says with an amused chuckle. He reaches out, ruffling JJ's hair. "What's your name?"

"JJ. And my Papa's name is Zander. We were on a walk when Papa hurt his foot."

My heart is up in my throat, hoping that JJ doesn't say too much. The last thing I need is for these hunters to learn about John and kick us out because we're a liability. Part of me is scared they'll want nothing to do with us, but part of me is scared they'll want to seek John out. I just want to be done with that chapter of my life.

"It's nice to officially meet you, JJ," Ronny says, holding out his hand. JJ shuffles me until his hand is holding under my front feet, holding my back against his chest as my feet dangle below. How embarrassing to be held like this by my six year old. He's lucky he's literally the cutest kid I know.

With his hand free, JJ reaches out and shakes Ronny's hand. "Nice to meet you. What's your name?"

"I'm Ronny," Ronny says with a wide smile. "And this is my friend Carlos. The big guy you saw with us is named Martin, the guy with the glasses is Cooper and the vampires with the babies are Axel and Jeff."

"Did you catch all that, buddy?" Carlos asks with a chuckle.

JJ nods. Then shakes his head. Then nods again. "I remember." That makes both guys chuckle again.

"It's okay, we'll remind you, JJ," Ronny says and my chest warms. The implication that we'll be sticking around long enough to remember everyone's name is there, just simmering under the surface.

"Let's get you two back into the RV. Do you think your Papa can shift?"

Carlos speaks up. "I'm pretty sure he's waiting for his paw to heal before he shifts. So it'll probably be a couple days still."

"That's fine. I promise you," Ronny says, looking me in the eye, "I'll make sure JJ is safe and taken care of while you're in your cat form, okay?"

My stomach flutters violently. As best as I can while quite literally dangling in my kid's arms, I give Ronny a nod. The smile I get in return warms my entire body. Gods, he's so handsome when he smiles like that.

The fact that Ronny knew JJ was the most important thing, that his protection and care mean more to me than getting out of this form makes me let out a grateful meow. Without knowing it, Ronny is becoming the true mate that I need in my life. Now I just need to get better so I can actually *tell* him that.

CHAPTER FIVE
RONNY

I STARE at the road ahead of me, doing my best to actually focus on driving. It's hard though when JJ is sitting in the seat next to me sleeping with his *dad* laying in his lap.

How did I accidentally pick up two shifters? What kinda luck is that?

I've listened to Cooper talk in depth about a deity that supernatural beings worship. Her name is Lady Fate. It's believed that she pushes those who belong together into crossing paths, one way or another. There's a tiny voice inside me whispering that just maybe, that's exactly what's happening here.

That can't be right, can it? I'm a *human*.

Maybe it's destiny that my place is to help these two. That must be it. Lady Fate saw two of her children were hurt and in danger and that's why our paths crossed.

I'm really glad that I was in the right place at the right time.

Without thinking, I reach over and pet the cat's head but immediately pull my hand back. I look over at him and give him a look of apology. "Sorry. That's probably weird now, huh? Like you're not just a cat. You're a whole ass person." My eyes dart up to JJ's, finding him still sleeping. It seems like most kids, car rides put him to sleep. "Sorry. I mean a whole person. I'm not used to being around kids, I have to be careful what I say."

The cat--wait, I really need to stop calling him that. *Zander* looks at me with bright green eyes, blinking slowly as I talk.

"Is it weird that I still want to chat while I drive? Do you wanna hear me ramble?"

Zander gives me a nod. He carefully stands up in JJ's lap, stepping over his legs and getting into my lap. My chest constricts with something I've let remain unnamed. He gets comfortable and looks up at me expectantly.

That's how we spend the rest of the drive, with me telling Zander about myself, about life on the road, about being a hunter. I even tell him about my video games filled with building random worlds. He lays there content, letting out the most peaceful purr I've ever experienced. It's a sound that lulls me and fills my chest with warmth. I know I've only just met JJ and Zander, but already I wonder what life would be like going back to not having them here.

I hope I won't have to find out anytime soon.

"So you're really a hunter?"

I look over at JJ, giving him a tentative smile. "I am."

"I've heard about hunters before," JJ says, picking up the bologna sandwich I've just made him and taking a big bite. "My dad used to tell me and Papa about hunters all the time but you don't seem like you're going to murder me."

Zander lets out a pained meow as I let out a surprised cough, not expecting something like to come from such a little kid. I rub my fingers through my hair, trying to not let my shock show. "Well, I can tell you with certainty that me and the other members of my team have no plans to hurt you."

"But you're a hunter and I'm a shifter," JJ says, looking at me like I've gained an extra head. "Dad says we're mortal enemies."

Zander puts his paws over his face, no doubt because he's embarrassed by the conversation, but I can't help but find the gesture incredibly endearing. "Hunters don't hurt shifters for no reason," I say slowly, wanting JJ to understand. "Our job is to protect innocent humans from supernatural beings and supernatural occurrences that try to hurt them."

JJ takes another big bite, his mouth completely full as he continues talking. "So if I don't hurt anyone you won't hurt me?"

"That's the gist of it, yeah. Does that make sense?"

He gives me a big nod. Then he looks over at Zander. "Can I play outside? Pretty please? I'll stay near Ronny's camper I promise!"

Zander looks over at me. "It's okay with me if it's okay with you. Carlos and Cooper are out there so they'll keep an extra eye on him."

Zander looks back at JJ, giving him a nod. JJ lets out an excited noise, shoving the rest of his sandwich in his mouth before running outside. I overhear him yelling at Carlos, telling him to watch him do a cartwheel. Affection floods through my core. The feeling hits me by surprise. I wasn't expecting to grow so fond of this kid in such a short amount of time.

"So your ex tried to scare you both with tall tales of rogue hunters? Is that right?"

Those big, bright green eyes meet mine. They're filled with sadness and hurt. I wish Zander would shift into his human form so I could hold him. I want to pull him into my lap and cradle him with softness and kindness. I don't know everything but I can piece a few things together. I have my theories and if they're correct, then Zander and JJ both deserve stability and kindness and so much more than I could ever give them.

Zander nods his head, giving me a little sad meow. My heart clenches for him.

"I promise you that you're not in danger with us. Jeff has some history with rogue hunters and would never allow any of his team to act like that. You're safe here."

Zander leaps from the table to my lap, bumping his head into my stomach. I run my hand over his back and he leans into the touch. It should be strange, petting someone I know is a man rather than just a cat, but I can't find it in myself to actually find it weird. I love this easy touch he lets us share.

Every hour I'm with Zander, I grow more and more fond of him. I long for the day he's able to shift. Will he be taller than me? Will he have gray tones in his hair like he does in his fur? Will he be flexible and lithe just like his cat form? My mind fills with images and ideas without my permission and I do my best to keep them PG. It would be strange to picture a man I haven't even met yet in various sexy positions, right?

I twist around in my chair, pulling myself over to my computer. I pet Zander one more time before getting to work, trying to find everything I need to know about this new case. I find out when these wishes started to happen, who was affected, where the wishing well is located, anything that'll help the people going into town to investigate. I lose myself in the familiar work, my eyes moving over my screen as I read the articles and random blog posts of the locals.

A questioning meow pulls me from my inner thoughts. I look down at Zander, finding him watching me with curious eyes. His green eyes dart between the computer screen and me, silently asking me what I'm doing.

"I'm making sure I have all the information I can find about the case we've taken. There was a wishing well that's basically come to life." I tilt my head to the side, doing my best not to think about my father. Magic like this can grant you what you'd like but at what cost? "Which is all fine and dandy until someone wishes for something terrible, like for their boss to stop coming into work, or for the lady who cut you off in traffic to get right-eous justice."

Zander nods along in understanding. I find that I like talking to him. I can say whatever I want without being judged or misunderstood. I wonder if I'll feel the same way when he finally shifts.

"Tomorrow morning the guys will head into town and check it out. Cooper is our lore expert. He has a book for literally everything. He seems to think it could either be someone with magic doing a ritual to make the well magical, or possibly a corrupted mage who's using the well as their home. Or in all honesty, it could be something completely unexpected. We won't know for sure until we start investigating."

I look down at Zander, finding those wide, green eyes still trained on me. I feel my cheeks heat with embarrassment. "Sorry. I could ramble all day about this stuff."

Zander meows at me and for some reason, I can just tell he's telling me that it's okay, that he doesn't mind listening to me. I smile down at him.

"How're you feeling?" I ask gently, my thumb running over his paw. "Do you think you'll be able to shift soon?"

I get a nod in response and my stomach swoops with excitement. "If I'm being honest," I say carefully, my voice soft, "I'm really looking forward to meeting you in person. I'm not sure why but there's just something about you. I umm, don't really have the words to describe it."

Zander paws at my thigh before shifting so he can bump my stomach with his head. It can't just be my imagination telling me this is his way of saying he feels the same way.

Gods, communicating with a cat shifter is *hard*. I can't wait until he shifts into a form that allows us to talk together instead of me just talking to him.

"Tomorrow they'll head into town but tonight we'll spend some time around the fire. Which leads me to a very, very important question," I say, waiting for Zander's eyes to meet mine. "Can JJ have s'mores?"

CHAPTER SIX
ZANDER

I PACE back and forth in front of Ronny's camper, nerves licking my stomach and making it hard to think about anything other than Cooper, Martin, and Carlos being gone. Everyone else seems fine. They can hold their nerves better than me. Maybe that'll come with time. Well, if I'm around long enough to get used to the feeling.

I shake out my fur, trying to get my racing heart under control. I've only known these people for a short amount of time but already, I'm worried sick as I wait for them to return.

"I can't believe I'm waiting here while the guys are out there investigating this without me," Jeff says, carefully moving a grate over the fire to start making lunch. My stomach gives a lurch of hunger that I pointedly ignore.

"Now you get a taste of how I feel every hunt," Ronny says with a snort and something inside of me releases. *Oh.* I hadn't even thought about the fact that Ronny usually stays here. I'm filled with relief all the way into my bones. I take a breath before beginning my pacing again.

There's something coming over me. Something I don't want to put a name to. My body doesn't feel right. It feels irritated and sensitive and like my skin is far too tight. I feel restless.

"How do you do it? I just wanna run after them and make sure they're okay."

Ronny shrugs. "Just think about it like an office job. You've delegated this task to one of your underlings."

Jeff makes a face. "I hate that."

"I knew you would," Ronny says with an amused chuckle.

Axel comes out of his camper holding Lily and JJ comes padding behind. Ever since meeting Lily, my son has been attached. I've never seen him around another baby before so I didn't realize the way he would absolutely fall in love. Every night he comes to bed, telling me all about what he and Lily did. Thankfully, Axel and Jeff don't seem to mind him tagging along behind them.

Last night JJ tried s'mores for the very first time. The way his face lit up with excitement was rewarding, even if the extra sugar meant bedtime was a bit of a struggle.

My entire body goes warm. These people have already accepted us. They protect us. They *care*. I do my best not to get my hopes up.

Just because Ronny is my true mate doesn't mean anything, not when the majority of the people here are a tight knit hunting crew.

I dig my claws into the dirt beneath me, taking my built

up frustrations out as best as I can. I hate this feeling. It's the unknown that's bothering me so much. I just don't know how Ronny feels, I don't know how these people feel, I don't know why I feel so fucking irritated today, and I don't know how the guys are doing that left. Gods, I hope they're okay.

JJ steps over to me and I weave myself around his legs, rubbing against him and marking him with my scent. "Are you okay, Papa? You seem upset."

Of course he noticed. I chastise myself, never wanting JJ to worry about me. It's my job as his Papa to take care of him, not the other way around. I let out a meow, letting him know I'm okay before going back to weaving myself between his legs, making him giggle. It's a good way to get all this access energy out of me that's seeming to build up out of nowhere.

Eventually, JJ grows bored of this game and heads back over to Axel and Lily. I'm left to my own devices once more which in this case, means my brain spirals back into anxiousness. I leap up onto the RV, laying down and watching the group around the fire. From here I have a good view of everyone.

My eyes leap over to Ronny, watching him work. He's got his laptop in his lap, writing something out. I watch his fingers skim across the keys. They're long and thin and work effortlessly. They tap away and I find myself growing warm all over in a less than innocent way.

Gods, what's gotten into me?

I don't even feel like myself right now. I feel out of control, like my brain can't focus on *one* thing before bouncing to the next thought. Yet, I keep coming back to Ronny. Watching him, smelling him, thinking about him. I want him.

I want him *so* fucking badly.

But it's better to realize that I can't have him now instead of letting myself hope. Hope makes it easy to be hurt. Hope makes you vulnerable. Being vulnerable isn't worth it, not after everything I've been through with John.

"You doing alright up there?"

My eyes snap down, finding Ronny standing there looking up at me. When did he even *move*? He looks worried. Great. I've managed to not only worry my child but also Ronny as well. Fuck, maybe I should just go for a walk so I can stop bothering everyone around here.

I give him a meow I hope translates into telling him that I'm fine but the look he gives me lets me know he's unconvinced. I shake my head, stretching my entire body out and meowing again. I carefully jump down with his help, bumping his leg with my head.

"I know you're worried about the guys but trust me, they'll be fine, Zander."

I bite Ronny's jeans, tugging on them for a moment playfully. He smiles down at me and relief so strong it threatens to force my shift hits me. That's when I realize that I *could* shift again. My paw is feeling a lot better, good enough for me to be walking around on two feet instead of four.

The realization makes me freeze. Do I *want* to shift? On the one hand, of course I do. I want to be able to talk to Ronny and meet him as a man. I want to be able to hug JJ.

But a small part of me is terrified. Things with Ronny are nice. He pets me and talks to me. But that's because I can't talk back. What if he sees me in my human form and stops having that easy camaraderie with me? What if everything changes once I shift?

I shake my head, doing my best to clear my thoughts. I bite Ronny's leg again before walking away, looking back at him so he understands.

"Oh, umm, are you going for a little walk?" I nod at him. "Okay, but if you're not back in 30 minutes I'll come looking for you, okay?" I nod again and if I could smile in this form, I would be grinning from ear to ear. He *cares* about me.

Gods, I hope that care lasts while in my human form as well.

I make my way down the path, finding the bathrooms. I look around, making sure no one is near before leaping up into the open window and crawling inside. The bathrooms leave a bit to be desired but they're to be expected for a campground bathroom.

I make my way into one of the showers. I stand there a moment, my mouth opening in a pant. Fuck. My body is so *hot*. I'm overwhelmed. Everything is too much. I can't stand being in this form another moment!

The shift hits me all at once. One moment I'm standing on four legs, panting and overwhelmed, and the next moment I'm on two feet, leaning against the shower wall.

I quickly turn around and close the shower door behind me, locking it up tight. Sweat drips from my forehead and my hands shake as I carefully turn on the water.

Something pings at the back of my head, something that should be glaringly obvious but I'm just not putting it together.

I've felt this way before.

My stomach sinks as the pieces begin to fall into place. I've felt this way before right before I went into heat, right before I got pregnant with JJ.

Fuck. I can't believe this is happening. I can't even ask my true mate to help me with this because he's *human*. Would he even understand? Would he even *want* to help me with my heat? I'm so completely and utterly fucked and not in the way I so desperately need.

I turn the water to cool, letting it wash over me. I let it wash over my head, running my fingers through my hair to keep it out of my face. It feels so good and the only thing that would make it better is if Ronny's thin, lithe fingers were wrapped around my--

"Zander?"

My entire body tenses and my ears pick up Ronny's footsteps. A whimper leaves my lips without my permission, letting him know I'm here.

Everything is growing fuzzy and I'm finding it harder and harder to remember why asking Ronny to get into the shower with me is a bad idea. It couldn't hurt, right? He *is* my true mate after all.

Right?

Gods this is suddenly so complicated. I let out a shaky breath and resolve to having this conversation and hoping somehow, Ronny can understand.

CHAPTER SEVEN
RONNY

I step back over to the group, ruffling JJ's hair as I answer him. "He went for a little walk."

JJ's eyes go wide. "Is he coming back? The last time we went for a walk we ran away."

My eyes jump over to Jeff's. We share a look of concern before I squat down to talk to JJ eye to eye. "He's coming back. I don't think your Papa would ever run away without you, okay?"

JJ nods slowly before smiling. "You're right. Maybe he had to go potty."

"You're probably right," I tell him, standing back up. So many thoughts rush through my brain all at once. What are these two running from? Or is it a *who*? What happened that they had to run? Whoever they're running from, are they looking for Zander and JJ?

Part of me would love to sit JJ down and ask him all the burning questions inside my head. But that feels wrong. I want to hear it from Zander, and only when he's ready to tell us.

A surge of possessiveness runs through me. I've only known these two for a very, very short time but already, I know I would do whatever it takes within my power to keep them safe. I feel a pull towards them that I just cannot explain.

It seems their past wasn't the best which is why I'm so fucking thankful I somehow stumbled upon them. They won't have the same type of struggles as before. I can't promise them the best life because I'm a hunter who's always on the road and helping with danger, but I can promise they won't have to run anymore.

Gods, here I am making promises to a person I still haven't even met. What's wrong with me and my giant bleeding heart? Maybe I should try waiting until Zander and I can actually talk before making grand, sweeping declarations.

There's a tiny part in my head that wonders if this is how Jeff felt when he met Axel but I quickly push that away. I'm *human*. Zander is a cat shifter. We're literally worlds apart. Aren't we?

"Hey!" Jeff calls out, "welcome back!"

I look up, finding Martin, Cooper, and Carlos walking into camp. They all look fine so today must have been somewhat smooth without any sort of catastrophic side effect happening. I will gladly call that a win.

Carlos has a pained look on his face and his eyes dart around. "Hey, umm, where's Zander?"

"He went for a walk. What's up?"

"I think--" Carlos cuts himself off, looking away. His cheeks grow pink as he tries to find the right words. "Well, I'm not sure how to say this delicately but I'm pretty sure he might need a umm, *helping hand.*"

Axel and Jeff look at each other before nodding. "Yeah, we smelled it too but we didn't want to say anything," Axel says. I tilt my head in confusion. "He probably went to take a cold shower."

"What are you guys talking about?"

Axel looks up at me with a frown. He lowers his voice so JJ won't hear. "I'm pretty sure our new friend is going into heat. At least, that's what it smells like."

The words play over and over in my head. Heat? Oh my gods. Zander is going into heat. I'm not clueless. I've read enough of Cooper's books to know what that is, but for some reason, the idea of *Zander* going through that, all alone, sends my nerves alight with *something.*

I should be there to help.

Wait, no, he wouldn't want that. I'm just a fucking stranger!

And yet, I feel myself pulled in his direction. "Okay," I say, clearing my throat when my voice breaks. My cheeks are bright red as I run my fingers through my hair, not wanting the guys to see just how this is affecting me. "Well, maybe I should go check on him? Just to make sure he's okay?"

Axel looks up at Carlos and the two of them share a look. Part of me is annoyed to be excluded but the bigger part of me can't think of anything other than Zander. He's all alone. He must be so anxious. I'll do everything in my power to make sure he's okay, even if that means guarding the bathroom door so no one bothers him.

"It should be fine," I hear Carlos say under his breath, "he's human so the smell of heat won't affect Ronny like it would a shifter."

"That's true," Axel finally says, turning back to me. "Go make sure he's okay but if he wants you to leave him alone, come right back." I narrow my eyes, feeling offended that Axel would think I wouldn't do just that. Before I can retort, Axel continues. "I'm sorry, I'm just being overly cautious, Ronny."

"I understand," I say with a nod. "Okay, I'll be back."

Martin gives a wolf whistle as I start walking towards the bathroom and I can feel my face heat so bright he must be able to see the red on the back of my neck which I confirm as true when the guys all chuckle. I give them the bird over my shoulder in response, pulling it back when I remember JJ is with them. Thankfully, he doesn't seem to be paying me much mind, too focused on talking to Lily who's sat in Jeff's arms.

I take my time finding my way towards the bathroom, assuming that's where Zander would go if what Axel and Carlos told me is true. What better way to cool off than with a cold shower? Although, how would he even reach the controls of the shower in his cat form? Is he lying in the sink, wishing someone would come turn the water on for him? I have to find him so I can help him, however I can.

The sound of the shower running hits my ears and my steps slow even further. Is that a random person? Or has

Zander shifted into his human form? My stomach flutters uncontrollably at the thought of seeing Zander in this form.

I shouldn't even be feeling this way! From what I can piece together, Zander is on the run from something or someone. He doesn't need some hunter catching feelings for him. And that's without even thinking about the fact that I've somehow gained feelings *for a cat*. What the fuck is wrong with me?

I rub my face with my hands, letting out a long breath. After steeling my nerves, I knock on the bathroom door. I hear someone suck in a shaky breath.

"Zander?"

There's a long pause where no one answers. I think maybe I'm bothering someone's shower. Just before I resign myself to turn away and keep looking, I hear a soft voice call back.

"Ronny?" That voice. Zander's *voice*. This is the first time I'm hearing it and it's *beautiful*. A shiver runs down my spine.

"Is that you Zander?"

"Yes," I hear back, Zander's voice breathless and barely there. He sounds worried and something inside me snaps, wanting him to know he's safe with me. I step into the bathroom, clicking the lock behind me to give both of us a moment of uninterrupted peace.

"Are you okay, Zander? I locked the door behind me so no one will be able to come in here and bother you."

"I'm okay," he says but I don't believe him, not when his voice sounds so *broken*.

"I won't take a step closer, okay? You're safe in here."

"I trust you," Zander says and that statement, said with such conviction, is the first thing I believe without a doubt. I warm all over, realizing Zander *trusts* me. "I know you won't do anything I don't want you to do."

"Can you tell me what's going on? You sound upset."

Zander snorts but the sound is anything but amused. My heart squeezes painfully in my chest. "I sound upset because I am, in fact, upset," Zander says, grinding the words out through clenched teeth. "I'm an omega, Ronny. I'm an omega shifter who's just gone into heat for the first time in like seven years. Do you have any idea what that means?"

I swallow thickly. My mind races with all the things I know about omegas. Zander must be so uncomfortable right now. Does he have an alpha? Is there anything I can do to make him more comfortable?

"Do you umm..." my words sputter out and I run my fingers through my hair, trying to find the courage to ask the question I want to ask. I'm not sure I want to know the answer but I know it needs to be answered. "Do you have an alpha?"

Zander lets out a shaky breath and the sound runs down my spine like warm water, pooling thickly in the pit of my stomach. "No," he breathes out, "there was John but he never bit me properly. He's *not* my alpha."

"Okay. Okay, cool," I say dumbly, cursing myself for the bone deep relief I feel. It's not my business that Zander isn't mated. It shouldn't make me happy to know he doesn't have an alpha. Gods, I need to get a grip.

The last thing Zander needs right now is me being a creep.

"Ronny?" Zander whispers, just barely loud enough for me to hear. "Why are you here?"

I lick my lips, deciding to tell the truth. "I wanted to make sure you're okay. I know we've only just met, but I care about you." My voice softens, "I care about you a lot."

"You don't even know me," Zander says back, but I can detect a hint of hope in his voice.

I rub the back of my neck, looking down at my converse shoes. "I don't understand it," I confess softly. "By all accounts I shouldn't feel this way. But I feel drawn to you. That's weird, right?"

"It's not," he says right away. "It's not weird at all." There's a long pause where all I can hear is the water streaming down in Zander's stall. Finally, he speaks again. "Do you know what true mates are?"

My breath stutters in my chest and my entire body freezes. "Yes?" I say though I know I sound like I'm asking a question instead of properly answering. I clear my throat. "True mates are two souls who are destined together. Lady Fate, the mother of the supernatural, destined them together and then does everything in her power to push them together. Is that right?"

"*Yes,*" Zander says and his voice sounds like liquid gold, washing over me and making my entire body somehow relax and tense at the same time. "That's right, Ronny."

I bite my bottom lip so hard I'm worried I might bite right through it. "Do you have a true mate?"

"*Yes,*" he says again in that same tone. The hairs on my

arm all stand on end and anticipation fills me. My hands begin to shake. "I have a true mate, Ronny. I do. And I need him so badly right now but I can't ask him to help me. I can't. He's *human* and this is too much to ask for."

"Ask."

"Ronny, I can't."

"*Ask*, Zander."

A whimper hits my ears and I look down at my jeans, finding them tenting terribly. My cock is rock hard and straining. Gods, I can't pretend this isn't happening.

"Ronny?" I hum, letting him know I'm listening. "You're my true mate."

I just barely keep myself on my feet instead of letting my knees buckle. Holy fucking shit. I'm someone's *true mate*? Lady Fate saw fit to bring me my very own soul mate? She's deemed me worthy of an instant-family? I'm overwhelmed. I'm breathless. I'm so incredibly turned on.

"Really?"

"Yes," Zander says right away. "And I know this is a lot. You don't have to help me," he says gently. "You can go back to the camper and wait for me there."

"I want to help you, Zander. However I can." My head is spinning. How can he be so sure? How can he know I'm his true mate? What if I hurt him? What if I can't actually help him during his heat? I've never even had sex before! How is some virgin gonna be able to help?

"I can smell that you're panicking. Talk to me."

I let out a frustrated noise. "How can I help you?"

"You can come in here and fuck me until I can't remember my own name."

Now it's my turn to whimper. As good as that sounds *in theory*, I have no idea what I'm doing. "I'm a virgin," I blurt out, ripping it off like a Band-Aid. "I have no idea what I'm doing. I'm sorry, Zander."

"That's okay. That's fine. It's okay. We can take it slow. We don't have to rush," Zander reassures, his voice soothing the worry I'm feeling. I believe him. But at the same time, he's in *heat*. I have to help.

"But you're in heat. I *want* to help."

"I'm gonna open the door, okay? You can step in here with me whenever you're ready. Or you can stay out there and keep talking, okay? Just having you here is helping, I promise."

The click of the stall opening is loud in my ears, a signal that Zander trusts me, that he's accepting me. I take a steadying breath, running my sweaty hands against the front of my hoodie before starting to take off my shoes. Part of me wonders the merits of just walking in there fully clothed but that doesn't feel right. I wanna be on the same level of vulnerability as Zander, want to come to him just as bare and open as he's being with me. That feels right.

I take my time, removing each article of clothing. I fold them neatly and place them in a pile near the door. Once I'm completely bare, I step towards the shower door. Just before I walk in, I pause.

"Are you still okay with this? I can go back to the camper if you want."

"I'm ready. You can come in."

I open the door and step inside, seeing my very *naked* true mate in his human form for the very first time.

Oh. My. Gods.

He's the most gorgeous man I've ever seen. He has dark hair, piercing green eyes, and the most beautiful treasure trail that leads down to a thatch of pubic hair. His cock is thin and pink and dare I describe it as *pretty*. He's shorter than me with strong shoulders and a tapered waist. He's perfect. He's so, so perfect. And I cannot wrap my head around the idea that he's *mine*.

Zander's full lips drop open as he stares me up and down. Both of our cheeks are red with a blush, taking each other in, seeing each other bare for the first time. It's overwhelming in the most fantastic way. This feels like nothing I've ever experienced before.

"You're beautiful," I say, my voice soft. I wonder if that's a weird thing to admit. Maybe I should tell him he's hot, or sexy. But the smile I get in response tells me I've said exactly the right thing.

"So are you. I've seen you without your shirt but seeing you completely naked is another thing entirely. Gods, Ronny, I want you so much."

"Really?"

"*Yes.* Do you want me too?"

I nod my head, biting my bottom lip. My cheeks are so hot they're probably making Zander's heat even worse. "I don't know how. I mean, I know how sex works obviously but, I'm nervous. I don't want to do anything wrong."

"You won't," Zander says right away, holding out his hand for me. I take it, stepping into his space but I don't quite touch him. Thankfully, Zander goes the last couple inches, plastering our fronts together. I suck in a sharp breath and my stomach flutters wildly. "Fuck," he whispers into my skin.

"This feels--" my words cut off because I don't even have the words to describe how good this feels. Holy shit.

"I know," he whispers back, kissing the front of my shoulder. "Is it okay if I direct you, would that be okay?"

"Please do, Zander."

He nods, nipping the skin he just kissed, making pleasure lance through me. "Wrap your hand around my cock. Stroke it the same way you would stroke yourself. I'm already on the edge of coming because of my heat so it won't be too hard to get me off."

"Okay," I whisper, my voice coming out shaky. "I can do that."

I reach down, wrapping my hand around Zander's dick. It's *hot* in my palm and I whimper without my permission. "That's it," he murmurs, his mouth moving from my shoulder to the underside of my chin, kissing softly. Then I feel his tongue come out, licking my throat and it feels *so* fucking good. I want him to feel as good as he's making me feel. I'm *compelled* to make him come.

I stroke him slowly, taking my time to feel his dick out, to find every ridge and vein. His cock feels so warm and soft and perfect against my palm. Someday soon I want to drop to my knees and feel his cock in my mouth, to see how he tastes against my tongue. But for now, I focus all my attention on touching him in a way that makes his breath stutter. Zander makes the tiniest moan and I chase that sound, doing the same thing over just so I can hear it again.

"Oh, Ronny," Zander breathes, his breath tickling the underside of my throat. "Ronny."

"I've got you," I say, wanting him to know what this means to me, that he trusts me. I might not know what the fuck I'm doing but I want this to be good for him, I want him to know that I'll be here to help however I can. I want to take care of him.

"Keep going. I'm so close. Fuck."

I grip him tightly, speeding up my hand slightly. His breath catches and the sound is like the most beautiful music to my ears. His precum wets my fingers and I use my thumb to caress his cock head slowly, pulling another beautiful noise from his lips.

"Ronny?"

I look down into those bright, green eyes I've come to know so well in such a short time. I tilt my head, hoping my cheeks aren't quite as red as they feel. "Yeah? Am I doing this right?"

Zander nods his head quickly, another breathy noise leaving him. "Yes. Very much so. This feels amazing. But I have a question."

"Ask it," I say, my voice thick with lust.

"Can I kiss you?"

My breath stutters and my cheeks somehow heat even more than they already are. I nod, a smile crossing my lips. "Yes," I tell him. "Absolutely. Please kiss me, Zander."

Zander gets up on his tiptoes in order to get face to face. He lets out a shaky breath that I swear I can feel in my chest before his lips barely touch my own. It's more like our lips are caressing than a kiss and yet, my earth is completely shattered into splinters before coming back together whole again with pieces of Zander embedded inside me. It's the most precious kiss I've ever been given and I know without a doubt it's only the beginning.

"Zander," I gasp against his lips before surging forward and kissing him again, this time harder. My hand continues stroking him, wanting him to feel good, wanting him to come. Wanting him to come *for me*.

Where is this possessive side coming from? There's a feeling welling up inside of me, screaming for me to be the source of Zander's pleasure. I've never felt like this but instead of shying away, I embrace it.

When Zander's lips open, I follow suit, following his lead. His tongue dips into my mouth and I'm lost. I'm completely swept away in emotions and feelings and pleasure. Nothing will ever feel like this again, nothing will compare to the feeling of Zander pressed against me, kissing me, tasting me. I might not have a full understanding of true mates but in this moment, feeling *addicted* to Zander, I start to *feel* what being a true mate means.

"I'm gonna come," Zander says, his voice cutting off with a cry. "Please, Ronny. Keep going. You're gonna make me come."

I keep doing exactly what I'm doing, not wanting to change a single thing and throw my rhythm off. Zander's face merges into the very picture of pleasure, his brows scrunched up, his bottom lip between his teeth. His hips chase my hand and it's the sexiest thing I've ever seen.

My own cock is rock hard, on the edge of finishing without even being touched a single time. Just watching

Zander move and moan and kiss me is enough to have me on the very edge.

"Oh fuck," Zander cries out moments before his cock pulses in my palm. I feel his hot cum hit my stomach and my groin, covering my cock. Fuck. I've never felt like this before, so out of control, so wanton. "Fuck. Ronny!"

I stroke him through his orgasm until he's biting my shoulder and squirming from aftershocks and over sensitivity. I finally let go of his cock, bringing my hand to my mouth. I'm not sure what comes over me but without really thinking it through, I lick his cum from my fingers, needing to taste him. Zander wants me with hooded lids, his cheeks probably as red as my own.

"Fuck, that was hot."

"Yeah?" I ask, self-consciously.

"Hell yes. Is it okay if I touch you?"

I let out a shaky breath. "You don't have to. This was about taking care of you, Zander."

"And I've been taken care of," he says with a smirk, gesturing towards his soft cock. "Can I make you come, Ronny?"

My head spins from how fast arousal hits me. I nod my head. "Yes. Please, Zander."

Zander smiles as he runs his palm over my toned stomach, collecting his own cum into his hand before using it to stroke my dick. Holy fucking shit. He's using his own cum to ease the path of his hand as he touches me. Why is that so fucking hot?

"Now you'll smell just right," he breathes, making my brain melt from how fucking hot his words are. It takes an embarrassingly short amount of time for my orgasm to take me.

"Zander," I breathe out, letting out a choked noise as I'm overcome with pleasure. Zander kisses me, biting my bottom lip as I come in his hand, adding to the mess on my stomach and groin.

"Gods," Zander says against my lips and I can feel the way he's smiling. "That was so hot, Ronny. You're perfect."

I'm not really sure what to say to that. No one's ever made me come before, no one's ever looked at me and saw *perfection*. Is that what having a true mate entails? Coming and compliments? Gods, I could get used to this.

"Thank you," I whisper, not really knowing what else to say.

"We should get cleaned up and head back to camp," Zander says as he gently lets go of my cock.

We both quickly use the shower spray to clean ourselves before stepping out of the shower. "Umm," I murmur, realizing we don't have towels. "This is... this is a bit awkward."

Zander chuckles warmly as he steps over to the automatic hand dryer, bending over and using it to dry himself as best as he can. We both try to fit under it which doesn't work, even a little. We end up giggling uncontrollably and I'm not sure my chest has ever felt so *bright*.

"I don't have any clothes," Zander says, wrapping his arm around his middle.

"Here," I murmur, picking up my pants and hoodie, handing them over. Thankfully, we stopped in town to grab clothes for both Zander and JJ before parking our RVs. He'll have clothes waiting for him back at camp, but for now, we'll have to make do. "You take these. I'll just wear my boxers and shirt back."

"Are you sure?"

"Positive. Let me take care of you."

Zander's cheeks turn a pretty pink color as he slides into my jeans. They're too long for him but fit for the most part around his hips. "I'm not used to this," he whispers, "someone taking care of me."

"Well," I say, pulling my shirt over my head and looking over at him. "Hopefully it'll become something that's second nature. I'm not sure how this whole true mate thing is supposed to go but already I'm attached," I confess softly. "I want you near me, I want you *here*. And I'm willing to put in the work it takes to be with you." Then I quickly add, "you know, if that's okay with you?"

The smile I get in response is the most beautiful smile I've ever seen. It steals my breath and makes my heart flutter within my chest. "That's very okay with me."

I take Zander's hand as we step out of the bathroom and start making our way back to camp. Gods, I hope the guys don't give me too much shit when we get back.

CHAPTER EIGHT
ZANDER

I squeeze Ronny's hand, still completely in disbelief of what's just happened. My heart is racing inside my chest, banging against the inside of my ribs. Ronny is holding my hand. Ronny knows that we're true mates. He's accepting me. Gods, he *touched my dick*.

Just before we get into camp, Ronny pauses. He turns towards me with a soft smile, one that fills me with warmth. Could this really be happening? Could I truly have this?

"How are you feeling?"

"I'm okay," I tell him seriously. "There will be another wave coming soon, but for this moment I'm okay."

"And when the next wave comes, what then? What do you need?"

My cheeks heat up. I'm not a blushing virgin. Hell, I quite literally have a child already. But for some reason, Ronny makes me feel like I'm experiencing all of this for the very first time. And maybe, in a way, I am. This time around things are soft and gentle and filled with affection. It feels *different* in the best possible way.

"I'll probably need to excuse myself to the RV. And umm," I clear my throat, licking my lips as I find my bravery. "And I would really like it if you helped me again?"

"Yes," Ronny says right away. His hand is shaky as he brings it up to my face, gently cupping my cheek. A small part of me wants to flinch away but the bigger part of me embraces his touch. Ronny won't hurt me, not like John did. I trust him. "I'll help however you need me."

Ronny leans down, placing a soft kiss against my cheek and my face breaks out into a wide smile. I look up at him through my lashes, really wanting to feel his lips against my own again.

"Papa!"

I pull myself away reluctantly, holding out my arms as JJ runs over to us. I catch him in my arms, picking him up and hugging him tight. "Hi, baby!"

"I'm glad you're human again. I missed you."

"I missed you too, JJ. Have you met everyone? Is everyone treating you good?"

JJ gives me the toothiest grin as he starts telling me everything I've missed. "I love Lily so much, Papa. I want a baby for our family! A little brother or sister I can take care of. Lily is so cute but she has to drink blood," he tells me, wrinkling his nose. I can't help but snort with amusement, listening as he rambles and rambles.

My eyes meet Ronny's over JJ's head and I find him smiling at the two of us. A soft smile that also has a hint of longing in it. My heart clenches at the idea of Ronny longing to be part of this, to be part of our family.

Ronny and John are complete opposites and that somehow soothes my anxiety over this entire situation. Lady Fate couldn't rescue me from John, but she saw fit to bring me someone who would be soft with me, to help heal the wounds that John left.

I'm terrified, but I'm also willing to let Ronny in. And as soon as my heat is through, I plan on sitting Ronny down and explaining everything that's happened to bring me here. But for now, I'll worry about taking care of myself with his help.

We make our way back over to camp. "Hey, guys," I say, waving at everyone. "It's nice to officially meet you now that I'm in a form that can talk."

Jeff stands up, walking over to me. He holds out his hand. "I'm glad you're feeling better," he says. "I'm Jeff. And before we get into anything more I just want to say that you're welcome here with us." The seriousness of the statement hits me full force and emotions threaten to choke me. "You're safe here. And I think it goes without saying that we're a family. A weird, mismatched family of fuck ups. Sorry, JJ, don't say that word."

"I won't," he says right away, making us chuckle.

"You're a part of that now," Jeff says softly. "And I want you to know that that's okay. You're welcome here, alright?"

I clear my throat, hoping my eyes aren't actually as watery as they feel. "Okay. That sounds good."

"Hopefully it's okay for me to say that," Jeff says with a

warm chuckle. "I don't want to step on any toes or put my nose where it doesn't belong. But Axel is very good at sensing these things. Plus," he says, tapping his nose. "There's no rush and no expectations. But I wanted you to know you're safe here with us."

"Thank you," I say, not knowing what else to say, unable to articulate what this means to me. "Thank you, Jeff."

He reaches out, squeezing my shoulder. The next wave of my heat is starting to make itself known. Add that with the emotions hitting me full force in the chest leaves me feeling overwhelmed. All I can do is smile back at Jeff, hoping he realizes just what his words mean to me.

"I hate to ask this since I've only just gotten back on my feet. Literally. But my heat is here. Would it be alright if JJ stays in your RV tonight?"

I can sense Ronny shifting nervously beside me and I reach out, squeezing his arm. His face is bright red and he's looking down at the ground. My poor mate. I'll do my best not to embarrass him.

"He's safe with us," Jeff says after sharing a look with his mate.

"Thank you," I say again, knowing that's the only thing I can add. The smile Jeff gives me tells me it's enough.

I nudge JJ's cheek with my nose, breathing in his familiar scent and letting the knowledge that he's safe soothe my inner omega. Heat nips up the back of my neck and my stomach clenches, letting me know the next wave of my heat is quickly approaching. I know these waves will keep coming quick and hard unless I get what my body so desperately craves, but is Ronny ready for that?

"Do you wanna help Axel with little Lily, baby?"

JJ's eyes light up and I can't help but smile so wide my cheeks hurt. He's already slotting himself into place with these people. I can't help but worry that the transition away from John will be difficult for him, but I'm happy to see him already letting himself be brought into this new litter.

He's still so young. Hopefully in the long run, he'll realize this was all for his benefit. That I ran so we'd both have the best life possible. I pray he'll see Lady Fate's hand in all this, guiding us to our new place. Our new *home*.

JJ gives my cheek a kiss before jumping out of my arms and running over to Axel. Axel gives me a soft smile, letting me silently know that he'll watch over my child the same way he would watch over his own.

I know I should have my guard up in place. I should be wary and worried. But I can't help but trust these people. Maybe it's my heat talking, or just maybe, I can sense Lady Fate's work in all this and trust Her decision to bring me here to these people.

Taking Ronny's hand in my own, I start to pull him towards his RV. He squeezes my hand, following along without me even needing to explain what's happening. I'm honored by the trust he has for me already.

"What's going on?" Ronny asks once we're in his RV. I breathe deeply, taking in the bright, lemony scent all around me, so concentrated here in Ronny's home on wheels. A shiver runs through me as my body warms all over. I suck in a shaky breath, trying to keep myself calm.

"Another wave of heat is hitting me," I tell him softly,

stepping back so there's a small amount of space between us. "Just like before, I'll need to take care of it."

"Let me help you," Ronny says right away. "Whatever you need, Zander."

"I need--" I cut myself off, running my hands over my face.

"Say it," he whispers, "whatever it is, I wanna know."

I let out a groan of frustration. "I want your cock," I confess, my face bright red when I say it. "But I don't want to pressure you or make you feel like we have to--"

Lips pressing against my own cut off my words. A startled noise escapes me, but the noise quickly merges into a moan. Ronny kisses me without an ounce of finesse but his enthusiasm is overwhelming in the best way. I sink into the kiss, my hands going to his face, keeping him in place. I never want him to stop kissing me. But at the same time I want so much more than just this. I want everything Ronny is willing to give me.

"Zander," Ronny breathes against my lips and I shiver again. When I open my eyes, I find him staring at me, his pupils blown with lust and his look that of someone *starving*. Like somehow he'll only be satisfied if he gets all of me, the same way my heat is making me feel about him.

"I want you," I tell him seriously, licking my lips and chasing his taste. "I want you so badly, Ronny."

"Then you can have me. All of me."

I kiss him again, starting to walk backwards towards his bed. Even in the midst of heat, there's no way our first time is going to be on the kitchen table. No. I want to take my time with Ronny and make our first time, *his* first time something memorable. Something we can look back at fondly.

I want to give Ronny everything I wish my first time was.

Inside his little partitioned bedroom, I begin to pull my clothes off. "Come on," I say with a smirk. "Get naked for me, Ronny. I wanna see all of you again."

Ronny quickly begins to strip, tossing his clothes on the floor with abandonment. It's endearing, seeing how excited he is, that blush ever present on his cheeks. Once we're both naked, I step into his space again. I look up at him, taking in the excitement on his face mixed with nerves. I promise to always take care of him. I might not be big or strong or a hunter, but I can still protect him. I can protect his heart.

"Kiss me," I whisper and a moment later, he does. His body presses against my own, lighting me up from the tips of my toes to the top of my head. My heat threatens to bring me to my knees but strong hands grip my hips, keeping me upright as Ronny kisses me gently.

I've only had two heats before. My very first one which I spent all alone, and the second that led to me having JJ. That one was rough. It was all about the fucking and knotting and biting. This time is different, I can already tell just from this one, soft kiss.

After kissing Ronny one last time, I turn towards the bed but he doesn't let me climb into bed, not yet. His arms wrap around my middle and he begins peppering kisses along my shoulder. He presses a kiss against the very back of my neck and my entire body locks up without my permission. As gentle as he's being, that spot holds bad memories for me.

"Are you okay?" Ronny pulls back and he sucks in a sharp breath. That's when I know he's seen it. Bite marks that John left behind. They're not mating bites, because it was never his intention to mate with me.

"Sorry," I whisper barely loud enough to be audible.

"You have nothing to be sorry about," he says back, squeezing me tight and pulling me so my back is against his front. "Is this umm? What are they called? A mating bite?"

"No," I confess softly. "Intention is important when it comes to a mating bite. John didn't want me to be his mate. He wanted kittens to pass on his legacy and I was the means for that. That's it."

Ronny's forehead drops onto my shoulder and he takes a moment to process this information. After another moment he kisses my skin softly. "Well, he sounds like a dumbass. I know we've only just met but I already know he missed out on a wonderful thing with you, Zander. You're a good father, you're strong, you're smart, and I'm really lucky that you're here with *me* instead of him."

There's something in Ronny's voice that makes a shiver run down my spine. He's possessive in the tiniest way and it whispers to my inner omega, it makes me feel claimed. I love it.

"I'm yours," I say, my voice coming out shaky and unsure even to my own ears. Thankfully, Ronny knows exactly what to say.

Strong hands turn me around until we're face to face.

Ronny leans down, rubbing his nose over mine before whispering against my lips, "you're *mine*."

For being a human, Ronny sure knows how to speak directly to my inner animal. I pull him onto the bed with me as our lips meet. As I lay myself against his pillows, we trade kisses. When our tongues meet, heat goes through me. My hips rise up off the bed, pushing our cocks against each other, adding to the anticipation and pleasure we're exchanging back and forth.

"Ronny," I gasp out, tilting my head back. Ronny's mouth moves away from my lips, trailing kisses against my jaw, then my chin, then down my throat. Gods, it feels so good and my heat is finally catching up to me, overwhelming me. I'm filled with *need*.

"What do you need, Zander?"

"Need you," I tell him through clenched teeth, pleasure zinging through me as he sucks a mark into my sensitive throat. My instincts are going wild at the feel of his teeth against me. They whisper *mark me, claim me, mate me.*

Ronny swallows thickly. "Do you need me inside you?"

A whine leaves my throat as my entire body breaks out in goosebumps. *"Yes."*

I reach down between us, plunging two fingers into my ass. I'm so fucking wet that they slide in with ease. After making sure I can take him, I pull my fingers out, using my natural slick to get his cock nice and wet.

"Fuck, Zander," he gasps out when I stroke his cock. "Fuck. I'm embarrassed to admit this probably won't last very long."

"That's okay," I tell him, my clean hand going to his face

so he'll look me in the eyes. "I just want you in me. I want you to come inside me. Can you do that?"

He nods vigorously. "If I do something wrong, promise you'll tell me? I want this to be good for you."

"It will be," I tell him seriously. "Because it's you. You're my true mate and that alone makes this special."

Ronny smiles wide, his cheeks bright red from the compliment and to hide it, he dips down and kisses me. The kiss is perfect and does its job, distracting me until all I can think about is how fucking wet I am, how empty I am, how much I want Ronny inside me.

"Please," I whisper, needing him more than I need anything else. A moment later, Ronny readjusts, the tip of his cock touching my entrance. I suck in a sharp breath, bearing down and letting him inside me.

"Holy fuck," Ronny hisses out and I let out a startled chuckle because *same*. This feels so good to be connected to my true mate like this, to have him fucking me, to have his first time feel like *this*.

"That's so good, Ronny," I babble, closing my eyes and enjoying the feeling of being full and stretched like this. His cock is fucking perfect, hot and hard and long. Gods, I could easily grow addicted to the feeling of him inside me. "Fuck. Fuck me, Ronny. Come on. Please."

Ronny buries his face against my throat, biting down on my shoulder as his hips begin to move. He pulls out before fucking forward, over and over. He starts slow, testing the waters, seeing what feels good. Very quickly though, he finds a nice rhythm and we both sink into it. It feels so fucking good and I close my eyes, letting myself get washed away in the feeling of his mouth against my shoulder and his dick stuffed tight within my ass.

"That's perfect, Ronny," I gasp out, my body clenching around him in pleasure as my orgasm gets closer and closer. "Keep going. Right there. Yes!"

My heart beats against my ribs, my body going tense. Ronny pulls back so he can look down at me, his dark eyes filled with lust. But they're also filled with affection. "I want to make you come so bad," he says, his voice husky. "Can I touch your cock? Would that help you come?"

I nod my head. "Yes. Please, Ronny. I'm already close."

Ronny readjusts onto his knees to have a better angle to fuck me from while also give him room to stroke my cock. He loses his rhythm but after a few moments, he finds it again. There's absolutely no skill in his movements, no finesse or fancy moves. But his enthusiasm and care make up for it. He truly wants me to feel good, he wants to please me, he wants me to come. Fuck, I've never had someone treat me like this and it's overwhelming.

"I'm gonna come," I blurt out, wrapping my legs around his waist and squeezing tight. "Keep going. Fuck!"

Ronny lets out a broken noise, his hand tightening around my cock. I can feel him coming. I can feel his dick throb inside my ass. I can feel the warmth of his cum hitting my insides.

My hips rise up off the bed and that changes the angle slightly. His cock rubs against my prostate and it's enough to have my own orgasm racing through me. I moan as my cum splashes from my erection onto my belly and chest, covering myself. The smell around the room is intoxicating and I sink into it, letting it wash over me and add to the pleasure running over me like warm water.

"Fuck," I whisper, letting my body go limp under Ronny. He lets go of my cock and I whimper.

"Sorry," he whispers back, carefully pulling himself free from my ass and I whimper again. "Are you okay?"

I nod my head, giving him the tiniest smile. "I'm okay. That was fucking amazing but I want to stay full," I admit with a blush. I want something inside me still as I come down from my orgasm.

"Like umm, like a knot?"

And now we're both blushing bright red. When I nod again, Ronny readjusts us so that he's spooned up behind me. I feel him take a deep breath before I feel something touching my hole. Ronny carefully puts three fingers inside me, keeping me full exactly how I need.

"That's perfect," I tell him softly, sinking against his pillow, my entire body content. I feel like I'm floating, completely at ease. "You're perfect."

Ronny kisses my shoulder again and I can feel the way he's smiling. "I'm just happy that I was able to help. And that, you know, it was good? For you?"

"It was very good," I tell him, wanting to soothe his worries. "It was so very, very good, Ronny. Probably the best sex I've ever had."

"Just because we're true mates doesn't mean I need my ego stroked."

I turn my head so I can lock eyes with him, giving him a serious look. "Ronny." He meets my eyes. "I'm not lying. That was the best sex I've ever had. It was truly perfect."

"Oh," he breathes out, a soft look coloring his features. "Okay."

Ronny holds me as I slowly drift off to sleep. When the next wave of heat comes, I'm not even scared because I know Ronny will take care of me. For once, I embrace the feeling and even enjoy it.

CHAPTER NINE
RONNY

"Well hello there lover boy!"

I walk over to the fire, knowing that my face is lighting up brighter than the actual fire burning in the fire pit. I sit down in the seat beside Martin, shaking my head at him. "Fuck you."

"No thanks. I'm pretty sure Zander did that well enough."

"Oh my gods," I groan, hiding my face in my hands. "I hate you so much."

"You don't," he says back, the two of us looking up when we hear someone else joining us. It's Cooper and Carlos.

"Glad to see you upright," Cooper says with a knowing smile and I hate them all. I hate them all so much. It would be so easy to use the skills I possess to cancel each and every one of their credit cards, flag their driver's licenses, and make their lives a living hell.

I let out a long breath, putting the diabolical thoughts away.

For now.

"I have no idea how long heats are supposed to last but his seems to be dying down for good now," I tell them, shrugging self-consciously.

"It can be anywhere from two days to seven," Carlos says. "This seems to be a quick one which means one of two things. One, Zander just has short heats."

"And the other?"

Carlos looks away. "Uhh, maybe I shouldn't say."

Cooper shoves his elbow into Carlos' side. "You already started, kid. Share the rest with the class."

Carlos lets out a long breath. "Right. So the other reason it's finished early is because he's caught."

"Caught what?" I ask, feeling so completely out of my depth. I really need to talk to Cooper about finding me some books about this stuff.

We all look at Carlos, waiting. Finally he winces and says, "you know? He's with child."

"He's with," I start to say but my breath catches as I realize what Carlos means. Oh. *Oh.* Zander could be pregnant. With my baby. With a baby we made together. Oh my gods.

"Are you okay?"

I look over at Martin, nodding my head. I quickly shut my mouth which has been hanging open. "I'm *fine.*"

Cooper snorts. "You look like you just saw a chupacabra for the first time."

I narrow my eyes at my friend. "That thing was scary as

hell! I can't be blamed for screaming, okay? And I'm scared right now," I add softly, rubbing at my eyes. "This is a lot all at once."

Martin puts his hand on my shoulder, squeezing it gently. "You're okay. It's okay to be scared. It's what you *do* while scared that matters."

I nod, taking that in and letting it soothe me. "I know what I'm gonna do."

"And what's that?" Carlos asks softly.

"I'm going to be the best damn true mate I'm able to be." The guys all nod, looking proud of me. Then I add, "but for the second, can you tell me about what I've missed with the case? I can talk through all of this with Zander once he's up. For now I wanna focus on the case."

Carlos looks like he's ready to argue but Cooper jumps in. "Alright, so as you know, the three of us headed to the well to investigate."

I lean back in my seat, letting out a breath of relief. "What did you guys find?"

"It's strange," Martin says, leaning forward in his seat, dangling his beer from his fingers. "There wasn't anything obvious. No signs of magic, no signs of weird tampering. It's just a little wishing well."

Cooper shrugs. "There were no weird markings or anything like that either. It's a strange situation." He takes a sip of his own beer, thinking about the whole situation. "I think we just have to do some surveillance and hope we get lucky."

"We could always try tossing a coin in."

I narrow my eyes at Carlos. "You won't be the one dropping a coin in. That's too dangerous."

"It's too dangerous to drop in a coin? Or it's too dangerous *for me*?"

"Yes," Martin says, nodding his head.

"You didn't…" Carlos just sighs, shaking his head in amusement. He might not be an actual kid but we all collectively look out for him. He's the baby of the group and it's our job to make sure he stays safe. "Fine, I promise I won't throw any coins into any holes."

"Martin? Maybe you and me can camp out in the food court this weekend. We'll take turns watching the well and see if we can't catch anything interesting happening?"

Martin takes a long swig of his beer and I can tell he's taking a moment before answering. I've always felt like there was something going on between those two. They bicker and fight but they also look at each other when the other isn't looking.

"Yeah, sounds good, Cooper."

"And if that doesn't work," Carlos says, holding up a quarter and smiling wide.

Cooper snatches the quarter away. "If all else fails, *maybe* we can talk about you flipping the quarter into the well."

Carlos does a fist pump to himself, making us all chuckle. "I have a feeling it's going to end up being something *weird* instead of malicious."

"What's weird?"

I turn around in my seat, finding Zander standing there. He's wearing my hoodie and shorts and I do my best not to let the guys see how Zander in my clothes makes me feel. I hold out my hand for him and he takes it, letting me guide him into sitting in my lap.

"This case we're working on," I explain, running my hand up and down Zander's spine.

"Ronny here doesn't think it's malicious. But we still have to be careful. We don't know exactly what the hell is granting wishes," Cooper says, readjusting his glasses.

Zander lets out a little yawn, looking absolutely adorable. And holy shit, I need to get myself together otherwise Martin will *never* stop teasing me. I clear my throat. "Call it a gut feeling," I finally say with a shrug.

"As a shifter, I was taught to always trust my gut," Zander says, looking down at me with a soft smile. "That's probably the same with being a hunter, right?"

"Absolutely," Martin says with a nod. "It's important to trust your gut out there because sometimes hesitating for just a moment is a moment too long."

"This job seems scary. Should I be worried?"

I shake my head and Carlos jumps in. "Don't worry about Ronny. He's usually the one staying at the base."

"Got it. So I'll save the worry I would use on Ronny and use it on you all instead."

Cooper snorts and I squeeze my arms around Zander's waist. "We've all been doing this for awhile," Cooper says with a wide smile. "We know a thing or two. The worst thing that's happened so far is our fearless leader literally dying. But it's fine," he adds quickly when Zander makes a worried noise. "He's undead now. And he found his true mate. So I call that a net gain honestly."

"For someone so fucking smart you sure are bad at reassuring people," Martin murmurs and here these two go again.

"I never claimed to be perfect, Martin," Cooper says, sipping his beer and looking away. "Some of us are good at reading but bad at words."

Martin just snorts in response. To ease the tension around the fire, Carlos changes the topic. "I'm not sure how you lived before," he says to Zander, "but I hope the idea of being out on the road is appealing to you."

Zander swallows thickly. He reaches down, taking my hand from his hip and lacing our fingers together. "The idea of traveling is nice. I like the idea of not being in one spot too long, if I'm being honest."

"Is there a reason for that?"

Zander nods. Part of me wonders if I should shut these questions down. Zander might not be ready to talk about all of this. We shouldn't push him. I open my mouth to do just that but then Zander is going on.

"I ran away. That's why we were in our shifter forms. I saw an opening to having a better life. For *JJ* to have a better life. So I took it."

Cooper leans forward in his chair, the mood around the fire flipping once more. Everyone here softens. "What were you running from?"

"My ex," Zander whispers, "his name is John. He's JJ's father."

"We don't have to talk about this, Zander," I tell him, kissing his shoulder. He turns towards me, breathing in my messy hair.

"It's okay. I don't want this to be some big, dark secret

that could possibly come back and bite me. I want to tell you. You're my true mate, Ronny."

"Awww," a couple of the guys all say, their voices synchronized. I roll my eyes, ignoring the heat in my cheeks at their chorus of congrats.

"I just didn't want you to feel pressured," I whisper against Zander's shoulder. He kisses the top of my head before looking at the other guys.

"John is a cat shifter just like me. When I had come of age, my parents basically gifted me to John. He was the leader of our litter. They thought they were making me the litter omega but John never actually mated with me. And I wasn't his only omega."

If I was a shifter, I know there would be a growl rising up inside my chest. But I'm only human so instead, I just tighten my arms around Zander.

"It wasn't a great place for us," Zander says softly and a lot of things stay unsaid. "I didn't want my son raised there."

There's a moment of silence as we all digest this. "Did he ever?"

Zander shakes his head. "He never hurt JJ. Hell, JJ's real name is fucking John Junior. But John wasn't a good alpha. He wasn't honorable. He wasn't kind. He ruled with an iron fist. He would have stifled JJ and stolen his joy eventually. I had to run."

"It's okay," I whisper, running my fingers through Zander's hair. "You did the right thing, Zander. And Lady Fate brought you to us. I think she knew what she was doing when she did that."

"I agree," Martin says and his voice is hard. "What better place to be than surrounded by hunters? You will *never* have to worry about that asshole again."

"I'm worried I'm trusting you all a little too soon," Zander confesses softly.

Carlos speaks up. "It's okay to keep your walls up at first. You deserve that after everything you've been through. But with time, we're happy to prove ourselves and gain your trust. Now that you're in this fucked up family, you're one of us and we protect our own."

It seems Carlos speaks the same language as Zander because I feel him relax against me. Zander nods, giving a grateful smile. "Thank you."

"Like he said, you're one of us now," Cooper says with a smile. "It seems our little family is quickly expanding. I think we might have to invest in another RV."

Carlos pokes Cooper's side. "Just think, it could be you next finding yourself a partner."

I don't miss the way Cooper's eyes jump over to Martin before falling to the fire. Cooper plays it off, letting out an amused snort. "We've been in this business long enough to know just about anything is possible."

Gods, I'll be glad when these two figure out their shit and either fuck already or fight once and for all. I run my nose over Zander's arm, listening to everyone chat. "I promise you're safe with us," I whisper so that only Zander can hear.

He turns his head, giving me a knowing look. "I think I understand, Ronny."

I kiss his arm and wonder how I ever lived life without

him by my side. I've known him for such a short time and yet I feel like I can't go back to what it was like without him here. My chest is so warm and so bright with him here and that's without even thinking about having JJ around, making me smile. Knowing these two people make me happy. I can't wait to continue to get to know them because I have a feeling, the more I know them the more I'll love them.

CHAPTER TEN
ZANDER

It's been a few days since my heat has faded for good. Ronny helped me through each wave of my heat, holding me tight, whispering soft things in my ear while I was overwhelmed with pleasure. It was amazing and I've found myself dreaming about the experience at night.

JJ has taken all of these changes in stride. He sleeps beside me every night, tucked against my chest while Ronny lays against my back. I'm sandwiched between the two most important men in my life.

I feel lucky.

Once upon a time, I wouldn't have dreamed of running. I would have been terrified of rocking the boat. I wouldn't raise my voice, I wouldn't stir the pot, I would be seen but not heard. Now I feel safe enough to speak up.

I keep saying it was all for JJ. I wanted a good life for him. And that's the truth, but I would be lying if I said I didn't dream of finding a shred of happiness for myself as well. I dreamed of my own personal prince charming that would save me. He would whisk me away from John and take me somewhere safe where I could be happy. Instead, I saved myself.

Any time now, Cooper and Martin will be back to camp to report if they've found anything from the wishing well. But right this second, I stand in front of the bathroom mirror, staring at myself.

I turn to the side, staring down at my stomach.

"There's no way," I whisper to myself, my hand going to the tiny swell I see there. There's no way, right?

The gestation period of a cat shifter is around two months, so when we find ourselves pregnant, everything goes *fast*. Including when we first begin to show.

I swallow thickly as I stare at myself. I already know the truth. I can smell it on myself. But knowing it and *acknowledging* it are two very different things. This changes everything. Even though everything was already changing. Oh gods, can I handle this after everything else?

I lean against the sink, getting closer to my reflection. I look into my green eyes, hoping my reflection will tell me what I need to hear. And maybe it does because instead of a deep frown and eyes laced with fear, I notice I have the tiniest smile. No longer am I stuck with a litter that worships a man that treated me like shit. Now I have a family, one who already cares for me, willing to do what it takes to protect me and my child.

"I can do this," I tell myself in the mirror and my eyes silently tell me that I believe the words to be true. I don't want to count this as a win yet, not when there's still so many things that are not certain. But I can't help but let hope bloom within my chest at the idea of being with these people, of being with *Ronny.*

I take my time heading back to camp, smiling when I overhear Martin and Carlos' voices. I find everyone sitting around the fire, the afternoon warm but not too hot that we can't enjoy a lit fire in between us.

"Papa! Come sit by us," JJ calls out, beckoning me over to where he's sitting on Ronny's lap. Ronny gives me a gentle smile, holding out his hand for me. I take it and he pulls me in, kissing me on the cheek. "Eww," JJ murmurs, wrinkling his nose at us and I can't help but snort.

"Oh," Ronny murmurs, "maybe I shouldn't do that. I'm sorry."

JJ looks at Ronny with a serious face. "Ronny, you can kiss my Papa as much as you want. But not when I'm sitting on your lap. Deal?"

Ronny looks shocked, his eyes going down to JJ's little outstretched hand, waiting for Ronny to make this a true deal. Martin chuckles and I look over at Jeff and Axel, finding them smiling over at our little unit with soft smiles. These hunters are so goddamn soft. I adore it. The atmosphere here is so different than my old litter, further cementing the hope inside me that this will work for the long run.

"I'll take that deal," Ronny finally says, shaking JJ's hand.

"So anyway," I say loudly, changing the subject. Carlos gives me a knowing look that I absolutely ignore. "Did you already tell everyone what you found? Did I miss it?"

Martin shakes his head. "Nah, we were waiting for you. I thought you'd like to hear how this all went down."

"Very much so," I say, waving him to go on.

Cooper leans forward with an amused look on his face. "Well, as you know, last night Ronny hacked into the cameras so we could check it out after everything shut down for the night."

"Right," I say, nodding along, remembering Ronny being up late on his computer. "So what did you find?"

"We decided it would be best to just jump down into the wishing well," Martin explains, "there was a trap door hidden on the side that we could crawl through. We followed the ladder down and found someone's home."

"You're kidding," I blurt out, completely enraptured in this story. "Someone's *living* in the well?"

"Yep," Cooper says, popping his P. "Long story short, there's a gnome living down there. He's old as fuck but harmless. We told him he had to stop twisting people's wishes or we'd kick him out of his house. He said he was too old to find a place that provided entertainment, free food, and unlimited coins." Cooper shrugs. "Fair enough if you ask me."

I sit back in my seat, letting out an amused chuckle. "So it really was some weirdo in the well."

Jeff laughs. "Not every hunt is something extravagant, thankfully. Sometimes we fight evil. But on good days, we just have to harass an old man into not using his magic for his own entertainment."

"Papa? Can I harass old men?"

I look over at my son, doing my best not to immediately

burst into laughter. My eyes meet Ronny's and we share an amused look. I take a deep breath. "Umm? Maybe it's best to leave that to the professionals for now, okay? Maybe when you're older."

"Old people get to have all the fun," JJ murmurs, pouting in my direction.

"Maybe when you're older you'll want to be a hunter," Ronny says carefully, rubbing JJ's back. "But maybe you'll realize you want to choose another path. Maybe you'll wanna be a firefighter. Or something stable, like an accountant."

"That sounds boring," JJ says with a wrinkle of his nose.

"The important part is that you can be whatever you want and this group will all do their best to make that happen, okay?"

JJ looks at Ronny for a long moment before giving him a big hug. "I love you, Ronny. I'm gonna be an astronaut so that I can go to the moon and look back at you being tiny as an ant. Okay?"

Ronny's face is overcome with emotion. He kisses the top of JJ's head before murmuring. "I love you too, buddy. And that sounds like a good plan to me."

Seeing them together like this threatens to bring tears to my eyes. They fit together better than I could ever dream. Maybe this shift won't be as hard for JJ as I feared. Apparently it's me holding everything up with my doubts and insecurities. Thankfully, these people don't seem to be going anywhere and don't mind me taking as much time as I need.

Jeff clears his throat and Ronny looks over. "So, have you found us something new?"

"I have actually," Ronny says, readjusting JJ on his lap. "I think we're heading to the coast."

"What's caught your attention?"

"There's cases of people going missing near the coast. But it's strange. They go missing for a weekend before seemingly being deposited back at the same bar they were last seen at with no memory of what happened."

"What are you thinking?" Cooper asks, looking intrigued. I can't say I blame him. I'm interested in knowing more too.

"My gut says a succubus. They could be seducing people, taking them for a weekend of feeding, before depositing their victims back at the bar. Possibly a mage who's capable of clearing memories. Maybe even some vampires, though there hasn't been any signs of bites so it's probably not that."

"Well check it out," Jeff says with a nod. He reaches over, lacing his fingers with Axel's.

"I've never been to the coast," Axel says with a smile. "It might be cool to have my toes in the sand for a little while."

"*After* we've finished the case," Jeff says, kissing the back of Axel's hand.

"Don't worry, I have no plans of getting myself into trouble again. But once everything is said and done, I'm sure JJ wouldn't mind swimming in the ocean for the first time either."

My stomach flutters with warmth, thinking about everyone thinking about JJ as part of the team. They think of *me* as part of the team. I reach over, taking Ronny's hand in my own, lacing our fingers together. He squeezes my hand, his silent way of saying he's here and that he cares for me.

I want to keep walls up high. I want to protect myself from being hurt. But the longer I'm here and the more I get to know these people, the safer it feels to let those walls down.

CHAPTER ELEVEN
RONNY

"Do you mind if I talk to you for a moment?"

Zander looks up at me and nods. I watch him as he kisses JJ's head before straightening and walking out of the bedroom. He pulls the curtain closed. It won't block out the sound of our talking but it'll keep the room dark to keep JJ from waking up.

I push out a chair for Zander and he plops himself down into it. I step towards my computer and then step back over to him. I run my fingers through my hair as I turn away again. I pace back and forth as my nerves get the best of me. Fuck. I shouldn't be freaking out like this. It's a kind gesture. I didn't do anything wrong. But what if Zander takes this as me trying to pin him down, trying to push him into something he's not ready for. Shit.

"What's going on?"

I freeze, slowly turning to face Zander. "Okay, so I might have gone a little overboard but I wanted to run something by you."

"Okay?" Zander says slowly, wrapping his arms around me and watching me with bright, amused green eyes.

I squat down so we're face to face. "I made some papers."

"Papers?"

I nod. "I've given you and JJ new identities." I stand back up, stepping over to my computer and pulling out the large envelope I was storing there. I hand it over to Zander and start explaining. "JJ needed a birth certificate so you'll find that in there. Also a social security card. Don't worry, I've done the same thing for Lily, it's all perfectly done and the government are none the wiser. I'm very good at my job."

I continue my pacing as Zander slowly opens the envelope, pulling the papers out. He's completely silent as he does it and it makes me even more nervous.

"You'll also find papers for yourself. You've got an ID in there, a driver's license, birth certificate, and social security card. I made up shit about birthdays and addresses and where you were born but if you want anything changed, all you have to do is tell me and I'll get them remade." I rub at my face. "And feel free to tell me this is going too far. I just wanted to make sure you're both taken care of. This is your ticket out, just in case. I never want you to feel like you're stuck. You and JJ can run again if you want but I wanna make sure you're safe and have the things you need."

Zander grabs my hand, forcing me to stop pacing. I turn towards him, waiting for his response. He swallows thickly. "Do you want us to leave?"

"*No.*" I shake my head, squatting down again. "I want

you both to stay here. But I don't want you to feel trapped. Right now I have all the power. But with these," I say, closing his hand on the envelope, "you can take back some power, you can have some leverage. You could leave if you wanted."

Zander lets go of my wrist and touches my cheek. I lean into the touch. "I want to stay," he whispers. "I want *you*, Ronny. This is the greatest gift you could have given us."

"I want to take care of you as best as I can. I want you to feel as powerful as I see you." Zander leans forward and I meet him halfway, kissing his lips gently.

"Thank you," Zander whispers against my lips. "I have to tell you something."

"Anything, Zander. Are there other papers you need? I can also get you a credit card in your new name."

Zander smiles wide and the brightness in his eyes steals my breath. Gods, he's so beautiful. I can't believe Lady Fate saw it fit to bring these two into my life.

"It's not that," he says, his voice colored with amusement. "You'll have to make some more papers though."

"Whatever you need."

"We'll need another birth certificate and social security card."

I nod. "Did you want a different name? A different birthday?"

"No. It's not for me, Ronny. It's for," his words trail off as he touches his stomach, his eyes looking down before meeting mine again.

I have a moment of confusion before it hits me full force

in the chest. Oh. *Oh!* Carlos was right. Zander's pregnant. Oh my gods, Zander is *pregnant*.

No words could describe the feelings I'm experiencing so instead, I reach forward and pull Zander into a slow, lingering kiss. I pour as much emotion into the kiss as I can, telling him how happy I am, how excited I am. I want him to know that I'm falling in love with him with every passing moment that we share. I will care for him and JJ and our baby. I'll be the best mate I can possibly be.

"Zander," I whisper, feeling overwhelmed with emotion. "I can't believe this is happening."

"Are you happy?" And it's the uncertainty in his voice that pulls at my heart. I need this man to know my feelings.

"I'm so fucking happy," I tell him, pulling back so I can rest my forehead against his. "I'm so happy that I've met you, I'm so happy that JJ is here with us, and I'm so fucking happy that we're gonna have a baby together. I never imagined anything like this when I thought about my future. It's so much more than I could have dreamed for myself."

I kiss his face over and over until he's giggling and pushing me away.

"And it's all thanks to you, Zander. I'm so proud of you for running. You could have stayed day in and day out but you took a chance. You made it to me."

Zander's pretty green eyes fill with tears and he lunges forward, tucking his face against my chest. I wrap my arms around him, holding him tight.

"I didn't even do it for me," he confesses softly and somehow my heart softens even further. This selfless man who would do anything for his child.

I kiss the top of his head. I'm overwhelmed with emotions right now. I'm so proud of Zander for everything he's done, I'm falling more and more in love with him, I'm realizing the lengths I would go to protect JJ, and now I'm coming to terms with having a baby. Holy fucking shit. I cannot believe this is my life.

"I'm so glad you're here," I say gently, "I want you to be happy here, Zander. And someday when you're ready, I want you to bite me."

"But you're human," Zander says, pulling away from my chest and looking up at me.

"I know," I tell him with a smile. "But I remembered you said mating bites are about intentions. So I was reading some books that Cooper gave me and there's nothing in there that says I have to have sharp teeth. It might hurt a little more than if I was a shifter but I should be able to bite you. Would you want that?"

Zander's smile takes my breath away. "More than anything."

"Then I will. I'll bite you and be your mate for real."

Zander kisses me softly, his excitement and happiness practically palpable in the room around us.

"You keep giving me gifts that I can't dream of repaying," he murmurs against my lips.

I swallow thickly. "You've given me enough just by being here." My heart speeds up and my hands begin to shake. "You're not the only one who's had to run. I understand."

"I remember you telling me you ran away from the little town you grew up in," Zander says softly, both of us sitting down, our hands connected between us. With his hands in mine, I feel strong enough to tell him about my past.

"As you know, there's something that happened to all of us, something that turned our paths towards the supernatural. There's a reason we're all hunters." Zander nods, squeezing my hands and encouraging me.

"My father was not a good man. He was angry a lot. He gambled a lot. He got our family into a lot of debt and my mother often just turned away, pretending not to notice all the damage he was doing."

"That sounds awful," he murmurs as he listens. Zander pulls my hands up to his mouth, kissing the back of them.

"It wasn't great. But my mother and I made it through the tough times. But one day, he came home and he was *different*. I still don't know exactly what happened, but I have my theories. I think he sold his soul, Zander."

Zander gasps. "You can *do* that?"

I shrug, pain lancing through my chest as I remember that night. "He was a monster."

"Did he hurt you?" I shake my head, but my eyes are sad. "Oh no," he whispers and I'm struck with how well Zander already knows me.

"My mother," I confirm. "That was the very first time I killed a monster."

I wait a moment, my eyes staring down at the floor. I'm not sure I can handle the look of distress or disgust on Zander's face. This is news that only the other guys of my crew know. I have blood on my hands and I would understand if that was too much for Zander to handle.

"You did what you had to do."

I tug Zander forward, kissing his forehead. Relief goes through me so strong I feel like I could cry. "I did. I still wonder if there was something I could have done. I had no idea the supernatural was even a thing back then. But now I would have found the person holding his soul. I would have tried everything."

"You can only do as much as you know, Ronny. You saved yourself. Without that, you wouldn't have been able to save *us*."

Emotion hits me full force in the chest. I needed to save myself in order to someday save my mate, to save our son. I never regretted that night, but it still felt uneasy and wondering if I'd done the right thing. I still don't know but now I have people around me that wouldn't be the same if I wasn't around.

I fought to find them without even knowing it.

"Thank you for listening. I hope this doesn't change how you feel about me."

"How could it," Zander says, running his nose softly against my own. "You're amazing, Ronny. And we're lucky to have you."

"I'm the lucky one to have you as my mate."

"Papa?"

We both look over, freezing when we find JJ standing there watching us with wide eyes. Zander holds out his hand and JJ walks over, crawling into Zander's lap.

"You're mates?"

Zander looks at me, wincing slightly but I just nod, letting him take the lead on this. It doesn't really feel like my place to say too much, not unless Zander wants me to. I might be Zander's true mate, but I don't want to overstep with JJ.

"Ronny is my true mate," Zander explains softly. "Lady Fate saw Ronny fit to be my perfect mate, baby."

"But what about Daddy? Are we ever going to see him again?"

Zander swallows thickly. "No. We won't ever see your daddy again."

"Daddy was mean. Wasn't he." It's not a question and my chest clenches, wishing JJ didn't understand that. He's too little to have the people in his life be unkind to him. The more I learn about this John, the more I want to absolutely *destroy* his life.

"Are you okay?"

JJ nods slowly. "I think I'll be okay. Maybe chocolate chip pancakes will help," he says seriously, making Zander and I snort with amusement. "If Ronny is your true mate does that mean he's gonna be my new dad?"

I rub the back of my neck, looking at Zander unsure. He tilts his head, letting me respond. "Well, buddy, I don't think I could ever replace your dad. But I'll be here for you however you want, okay?"

JJ takes my hand. He partially shifts one of his nails into a claw and my eyes widen. Zander pulls JJ's hand away. "What are you doing?"

JJ looks at Zander like he's grown another head. "Blood oath? Duh?"

Zander sputters. "Where did you hear that word?"

"I don't remember. Maybe Daddy? Maybe Lily," he says with a nod.

"Lily? The baby?"

"Yes. She drinks blood. She knows about blood oaths, Papa. Trust me. I want Ronny's blood so he's stuck with us forever."

I take JJ's hand in my own. "We don't need a blood oath for that, buddy. Nobody knows what the future holds but we trust that Lady Fate knows what's best, right?" When he nods I go on. "And I have a feeling that means you'll be here with me and the rest of the crew until you're old enough to start making your own decisions. How does that sound?"

His face breaks out into a giant smile and he jumps from Zander's lap into mine. I hold him tight. I don't want to admit it out loud but I already see JJ as my own. I'll do everything in my power to protect him and make sure he's safe and happy. "I love you, Ronny."

"I love you too, JJ."

"Alright, mister," Zander says, picking up JJ and heading back towards bed. "You're up way past your bedtime." JJ whines, complaining that he's not even a little bit tired which falls flat when he ends up finishing his sentence with a giant yawn.

My heart is so full as I watch *my mate* put JJ back into bed.

CHAPTER TWELVE
ZANDER

MARTIN FLOPS into his seat beside the fire, letting out a long and tired groan. Frustration radiates off of him in waves and I wince with sympathy.

"Still nothing?"

"Not a damn thing! You'd think after tracking this fucking case for a month and a half we would have caught some sort of break by now but whoever is in charge of these abductions is slippery as fuck!"

I run my hand over my round stomach, listening to Martin rant. This isn't the first time I've heard this rant, far from it really. Martin and Cooper have taken the lead on this case, wanting to give Jeff and Ronny some time to get used to having their families on the road. Which is really sweet, but also, I think it's time the entire group helped with this case before these two self-destruct and kill each other.

When we first got to the coast, I had high hopes for Martin and Cooper putting their differences aside and truly working together for this case. And at first, that's exactly what they did. But as the weeks went by with no results, the bickering and the pissing contests started happening.

When will they realize they're simply on different sides of the same coin?

"Have you thought of taking a week off and coming back to the case with clear heads?"

Martin stares at me for a long moment. "And if the trail runs cold? What then?"

The little one inside me jumps, bumping against my hand and a soft smile plays at my lips despite the conversation we're having. "Isn't it already cold? In a way, at least? You're coming up short and chasing this case by the tail. You're like a dog who's sure this time you'll catch it," I say with a snort.

"First of all, rude," Carlos says, sitting beside me. He looks at my stomach with giant puppy eyes and I nod, giving him permission to touch. "Second, I think Zander might be right. We're chasing our tails here. They somehow have one up on us. It might be best to lay low for a little bit. Give them the sense we're no longer chasing them and wait for them to strike again."

"That's one more innocent person being taken," Martin says in frustration.

Carlos' hand connects with my belly and the baby kicks him. I swear, these two are already thick as thieves and they haven't even officially met yet.

"The people being taken aren't being hurt," I say hopelessly. I'm not trying to play devil's advocate in the slightest but I also can't sit back and watch these two work themselves into the ground if I can help it. "Give it one week of rest and then we'll all jump into the case with both feet."

Martin crosses his arms over his chest. "Looks like I'm outvoted anyway," he says with a heavy sigh. "I realize I'm not the brains of this operation but something about this one feels urgent. I feel like this is where we're supposed to be."

Cooper comes over to join us by the fire, looking just as exhausted as Martin. "If I have to hear you say that phrase one more time," he says tiredly.

"What?" Martin asks, his brows drawn low. "It's the truth. You're obviously the brain."

"You're super smart," Cooper says and I can tell this isn't the first time he's said this. I can't stop myself from smirking. "Just because you're also built like a brick wall doesn't mean you're stupid. You've gotta stop thinking like that."

"Whatever," Martin grits out through clenched teeth. "These guys want us to take a week off. It feels wrong."

I look over at Cooper, watching conflicted emotions flash behind his glasses. "I get what you meant before. This one *feels* different," he says, touching the center of his chest.

My eyes meet Carlos' and we share a look. There's something going on here, something that their instincts are clearly reaching for. Will they allow themselves to follow those instincts or will they try to push them away? Being hunters, maybe they won't be like most humans, maybe they'll know to channel those feelings and let them lead them.

"One week," Martin finally says, the fight going out of

him. "One week. And I refuse to do it completely unplugged. I want Ronny monitoring things and informing us if anything changes. But otherwise, we won't be jumping from bar to bar and chasing every tiny lead we get. One week and then we all jump in. Deal?"

"What's the deal?" We look up, finding Axel and Jeff standing there. "I'm just kidding. I heard the whole conversation." Jeff points at his ear and smiles. "One of the perks of being a vampire."

"Is Lily sleeping?"

Axel holds up a baby monitor and nods. "She was really fighting it today, but I finally talked her into napping."

"What I'm hearing is that you guys don't even need me anymore," Jeff says with a giant pout that turns into a grunt when Axel elbows him in the stomach. "I'm kidding. But seriously, I think taking a little break would do you both some good. We'll hit the ground running next week."

I'm sure the conversation is over but Jeff is clearing his throat. "And I just want to add that I'm sorry."

"What?"

Jeff rubs the back of his neck. "Ever since I was turned, I worry I'm not here for you all the way you need. And before you argue, don't. I know I've been taking a backseat lately, trying to find my legs. I've got Axel and Lily now but that doesn't stop me from also being your leader. I want the best for you all and the best for this team. I want to keep this world in order because now I have a daughter growing up in it. That gives me extra motivation. So from now on, I'll be a bit more hands on and if I need to step back because of family time, I'll communicate that better. Okay?"

There's nothing to really fight about so everyone here nods and gives noises of agreement. With that, Jeff nods his head and sits down.

"Also, I ordered pizza. A local place said they would deliver here at the campgrounds and I figured we could all use a treat." Beside me, Carlos' stomach growls.

Eventually, JJ and Ronny get back from their walk. JJ runs over to me, carrying a handful of random flowers they've collected while out on their walk. My heart warms as my son tells me all about the animals they saw and the things they've collected.

My eyes jump up to Ronny's, finding his dark eyes already on me. He's so soft with us, making sure we're cared for and loved. Loved. He loves us.

I love him.

I've known for awhile but with everything changing so fast, I was afraid to admit it out loud. Ronny is *human* after all. Shifters fall for their true mates supernaturally fast. Almost instantly. But humans prefer more of a slow burn as far as I know and I was scared of frightening him away with yet another shifter *thing*.

But in this moment, with his soft eyes on me, I know without a doubt that Ronny loves me. And I love him. There's no more reason to hold myself back.

So I don't.

Leaning over, I give Ronny a soft, lingering kiss. When I pull back, there's a little smile playing at his lips, his scent lemony and bright. I finally admit to myself that I want Ronny to be my mate in every sense of the word. I want him to leave a bite in my skin that declares me as his. I want to be claimed just as much as I wish to claim him.

I look over at Jeff and Axel. "Would you mind if JJ stays over with you guys tonight?"

Axel looks at me, his brows rising in surprise when he sees the look I'm giving him. "Absolutely. I'm sure he'll love helping me with Lily."

"I get to sleep over with Lily?"

"You do," I tell him with a wide smile. "Does that sound like fun?"

"Yes! I love Lily. And I love my baby sister," JJ says, leaning down to kiss my stomach.

"We don't know if they're your brother or sister yet, JJ."

JJ's brows wrinkle. "I know, Papa. Trust me. My sister is in there."

Ronny reaches over, ruffling JJ's hair. "I trust you, buddy."

"You should be more like Ronny, Papa," JJ murmurs under his breath, making us all chuckle. My chest is so full and so warm. Is this what having a litter is actually supposed to feel like? I almost feel bad for John and his following because they'll never experience anything like this. But then again, that's their choice I suppose.

"Do you have plans for tonight?" Ronny asks, leaning over to whisper in my ear. A shiver goes through me at the feel of his hot breath.

"I do. Is that okay?"

He nods, giving me a smile. "Of course, baby. I trust you."

That warmth in my chest is back full force, whispering

that my decision is a good one. Ronny is my true mate, but more than that, he's proven himself to be a good match for me. Lady Fate might have brought me to him but he put the work in and brought my walls crumbling down. She pushed me in the right direction but Ronny was waiting there with open arms for me.

I sit back in my chair, snuggling my child against my chest, listening as everyone talks about going to the beach tomorrow. It'll be a fun filled day but tonight, I have plans to finally make Ronny mine.

CHAPTER THIRTEEN
RONNY

I PULL Zander against me once we're alone inside my RV. A shiver runs through me as his belly touches my own. I still have a hard time wrapping around my head that my baby is in there, nestled safe and warm. Zander's pregnancy has been so incredibly fast, so I've had to prepare myself quickly to become a father.

Maybe it's better this way. Less time to overthink things.

His fingers play through the hair at the back of my neck before he's tugging me down into a kiss. I let him lead me, opening my lips for him when I feel his tongue press against the seam of my lips. A moan leaves my throat when our tongues touch. A shiver runs through me at the fierceness of Zander's kiss. He's usually so gentle with me, making sure I'm okay. It makes me happy to know he trusts me enough to take exactly what he wants, knowing I'll ask him to slow us down if I need it.

"I want to tell you something," Zander whispers against

my lips. He helps me out of my shirt, his hands running over my toned chest and stomach.

"Anything."

"I love you."

Surprise rushes through me before I go warm all over. A smile splits my face so wide that my cheeks hurt. Holy shit. Of course I love Zander, how could I not. But it overwhelms me that he could somehow love me back.

"I love you, too," I say right away, cupping his face gently in my hands. I kiss his nose and he smiles. "I love you so much. I love you and JJ and our baby."

We kiss again and this time it's much gentler. "I have one more thing," he says with a warm chuckle. "I want you to be my mate, Ronny. I'm ready to finally take that step."

"Are you sure?"

"Yes," he says right away, nodding his head. "I trust you, Ronny. I know you'll protect me and push me and make sure JJ and this baby are okay. I love you, Ronny. I want you as my mate."

"Then we'll make it happen. But you'll have to talk me through it."

"Of course," Zander says, his hands tightening around my wrists. "I'm happy to talk you through everything."

We quickly strip out of our clothes, our hands caressing each other and our mouths finding each other's skin. Everything feels heightened, electrified with emotion now that our intentions have been stated. I'm going to be Zander's *mate*.

Zander lays on his back, his thighs open for me. I smile wide as I lay on my stomach between his open legs. "Is this okay?" I ask him, making my plan very obvious. He licks his lips, staring down at me with lust filled eyes, nodding his head.

With permission, I take his cock into my mouth. The feel of it against my tongue makes my own cock throb. I love this. I love the taste, love the feel, love how powerful it makes me feel to pleasure Zander like this.

A moan rings through the room and I just barely keep myself from smiling. At the same time, I bring my hand to his ass, swirling my finger around his wet hole. He squirms, wordlessly begging for what he wants and of course I give it to him.

"Ronny! Oh fuck," Zander gasps out as I finger him, taking my time and making sure he's nice and ready for my cock. I've only been having sex for a few months but I like to think I'm a fast learner and Zander makes it easy and fun, always willing to take things as fast or as slow as I need.

I'm lucky to have him as my mate.

I get lost in the act of pleasuring Zander. My hips ride down against my mattress and I moan, and based on the way Zander's hand finds my hair and *pulls*, I'd say it must feel really, really good on his dick. He gasps out, his eyes wide as he stares down at me.

"Ronny. Please. I want you to fuck me. Please."

I pull my mouth away from his cock. The only thing keeping my disappointment at bay is knowing I'm about to be inside him. Knowing I'm about to become Zander's mate in more than just name makes my stomach flutter with excitement. Will I be able to tell the difference? Will I be able to feel him like other mates sense each other?

"Do you wanna ride me? So you're in control, baby?"

Zander's cheek pinken and he bites his bottom lip. "Actually, I was hoping you would take me from behind? I want you to bite the back of my neck."

Shock makes me freeze. That area, the spot that John bit over and over but never made Zander his mate is quite literally a tender spot, not only physically but emotionally. "Are you sure?"

"I'm tired of that being this heavy cloud hanging over my head. I want you to be mine. I want you to cover up his marks. Would you?"

"Yes," I tell him, crawling up his body and kissing him. I'm careful of his belly but still keep us skin to skin. "I love you, Zander. You're mine."

I kiss his cheek. "I have to tell you something, and I'm worried this is going to quite literally ruin the mood but I think you should know."

"Okay?"

"John will never be a problem again."

Zander blinks slowly, taking this in. "What did you do?"

"I've ruined him," I say bluntly. "And I feel zero remorse."

"But how, Ronny?"

"I flagged his ID, he'll never be able to have a credit card or get a loan, no bank will give him the time of day, when he applies for jobs his name will be flagged." I swallow thickly. "He's on a no fly list, I've made it so the IRS is looking into his finances and I'm pretty sure they'll be arresting him for tax fraud at the least. Even if nothing sticks he will never be able to have a normal life again. There's no way a litter would allow such an alpha as their leader. He's ruined."

I get it all out, praying that Zander will still want to be my mate after hearing what I'm capable of.

"Really?"

I stare into his hopeful, green eyes. "Yes."

I wasn't sure what I was expecting but being flipped over onto my back and kissed within an inch of my life was not it. I let out a startled noise before I begin to kiss Zander back. I can tell he's relieved, but I need him to say it.

"Was that okay?"

"I'm so relieved," he confesses softly. "I won't have to worry about him again. Can you track him? Just to keep tabs on him and know where he is?" I nod and in response, I'm gifted even more kisses.

Our kisses quickly fill with heat. Zander rearranges, getting onto his hands and knees. I'm so used to making love face to face. Seeing the bite marks left behind fills me with unease, but I push that away, determined to make Zander feel good as I make him my mate once and for all.

"Please," Zander whispers, pushing his hips up into the air. "Fuck me, Ronny."

I grip Zander's hip with one hand, my other guiding my cock to his hole. His whimper makes a shiver run down my spine as the head of my dick catches on his rim. Fuck, he's so wet and so warm.

Matching groans leave us as my cock finally enters

Zander. I push forward, going achingly slow until my hips are pressed against his ass.

"Fuck," I gasp out, just savoring the feeling of Zander so warm and tight around me.

"Come on," Zander whines, reaching back and slapping my hip. "Fuck me, Ronny. Don't hold back."

I lean forward, plastering my chest against his back as I fuck him. Gods, he feels so fucking good. I mouth along his shoulder, loving each and every sound he makes. I'm addicted to making him feel good.

"I'm so close," he says, leaning his face against his pillows. "Come with me, Ronny. Come inside me. *Fuck!* I want you to bite me."

My cock *throbs* inside of Zander's ass as I fuck him. I kiss the back of his neck. Right here. This is the spot. I'm not sure if I have some inner instinct I'm channeling or if I'm completely off course but as pleasure crashes over me like waves, I bite Zander. My teeth clamp onto the back of his neck and I bite down as hard as I can.

Mate. Mine. Zander. Us. Mine. Mate.

A whimper escapes my throat as I taste blood. I let go, looking down with wide eyes as I see a bloody bite on the back of Zander's neck.

Zander's ass clamps down around my cock as he's overcome with pleasure. Fuck. Another shiver wracks through my body. I carefully pull out and readjust us until I'm on my back and he's in my lap.

"Want you to come and bite me too," I murmur, planting my feet on the bed so I have leverage to thrust up into Zander's body. I've already come but the adrenaline of mating has apparently helped me stay hard a little longer than usual.

Zander nods, wrapping his hand around his cock and stroking himself as he leans down and plants a kiss against my shoulder. There's a moment where I wait in suspense. And the next Zander is moaning before pain lances through my shoulder.

"Gods! Fuck!"

Our mating becomes cemented in that moment. I can feel him. I can sense that he's my mate, that he's mine. It's like nothing I've ever experienced before.

"Mine," I whisper, tucking Zander against my chest and peppering kisses into his hair. "You're mine."

"I'm yours and you're mine," he says back with a wide smile. We kiss and I wrinkle my nose. Now that everything is said and done, it's kinda gross that I can taste our blood on our tongues like this.

"Let me go grab supplies to clean us up and then I promise you can have all the kisses you want."

Zander giggles, nodding his head and slapping my butt as I walk away. If this is what I look forward to for the rest of my life, then gods, I am one lucky man.

CHAPTER FOURTEEN
ZANDER

OUR DAY at the beach unfortunately is postponed. Thankfully everyone is extremely understanding on account of *me literally going into labor!*

"Ouch, ouch, ouchie," I murmur sadly, my body going tense all over. I look over at Ronny, narrowing my eyes at him.

"I'm sorry, baby," Ronny says, wrapping his arms around me and running his hands up and down my back. It helps soothe some of the pain lancing through me. "I wish I could do more."

"It's fine," I force myself to say. "I've been through this once before. I can handle this."

"Thankfully," Jeff says, popping his head into our RV, a smile stretching across his face. Gods, I wanna scratch the smile right off his stupid face. How dare he look so happy while I'm in so much pain. "You won't have to do this alone."

I stop the growl that's half formed inside my chest. I

take a deep breath, breathing in Ronny's lemon scent and letting it calm me down. It wouldn't be okay to hurt my family. I'm sure they'd forgive me but I would never forgive myself.

"What do you mean?"

"Would it be alright if I came inside?" The voice outside belongs to someone feminine and a small part of my brain registers it as someone I've met before. My inner omega doesn't raise his head in alarm, instead sending me senses of peace that she's here. I trust that inner voice.

"Come on," I call out, watching as a short woman steps in, her hair snow white but for a streak of seafoam green in the front. She smiles at me, her eyes soft yet somehow all knowing. I remember her from Axel's home, the same day Ronny found JJ and I.

"Hello," she says softly, stepping into the bedroom area where Ronny and I are standing. His arms tighten around me but his scent stays steady, trusting this woman in my space and that further relaxes me.

"Star, right?" Ronny asks.

"That's right. And you're Ronny and your mate here is, Zander." I nod. "I've helped a lot of omegas bring their babies into the world and I'd be honored to be leaned on if you needed help as well."

"Thank you," I murmur, feeling a bit out of my depth. "In my old litter, we didn't really have anyone to help us. We just kinda locked ourselves into a closet until it was over."

Ronny stiffens beside me and I wince. He kisses the top

of my head, silently letting me know that it's okay and I won't ever have to experience that again.

My eyes move to Ronny's shoulder where my mating mark is left. He took the bandages off this morning and it's healing up really nicely. He's mine and I'm his. I've been through so much in the past but that's exactly what that is, my past. Ronny, JJ, this baby and this crew, they're my future.

"I would love your help," I say, smiling at Star. My smile quickly fades away as my stomach cramps up. Another contraction wracks through me and I grit my teeth. "Fuck."

Star looks over at Ronny. "Alright, your mate needs you. Let's get this kitty relaxed and ready to bring your kitten into the world."

Between the two of them, they get me in bed with warm blankets wrapped around me. Normally, I would be over-heating but there's something very primal about making a nest around me. It speaks to my inner cat.

"I need more of your scent," I murmur from beneath my mountain of blankets. "Take off your shirt."

"I could grab one--"

"No. Absolutely not. I need the one you're wearing right now."

"Seriously?"

Star clears her throat, raising her brow at Ronny. Ronny lets out a sigh and starts stripping out of his shirt.

"Yes, thank you," I say, grabbing his shirt and burying my face against the fabric. Oh gods, this is so perfect.

Another contraction goes through me and this one flows over me. I can feel my body preparing for our baby's birth but this time I'm not fighting against the pain, I work with it.

"I think you should get under there with him," Star suggests. "It's just about time to start pushing and he'll want you close."

Ronny shimmies his way under the blankets with me. His warmth and scent cling to me, settling my inner omega. There's pain and heat and pressure, but at the same time I feel acceptance and love and cared for. This is such a stark difference to JJ's birth.

I lay on my right side with Ronny spooned behind me. He carefully lifts my left leg into the air while Star sits at the end of the bed. This is perfect. I'm comfortable and surrounded by Ronny.

"You're doing so well," Ronny whispers into my hair. "You've got this, Zander."

I nod along to his words, concentrating on my body. When I feel the need to push, I bear down with everything I have. I'm not sure how long we do this, breathing through the pain and pushing when my body tells me. It could be minutes. It's more likely it's hours.

"Come on," Star says, her voice spurring me on. "They're right here. Give me one more giant push."

I grit my teeth and give this push everything I have.

"There she is," Star murmurs as my entire body goes slack with relief. It took so much to get her out but now that she's here, my body finally relaxes. Ronny is gentle as he helps me sit up, staying near and helping me hold our daughter for the first time.

"She's beautiful," I murmur, looking down into bright

green eyes that match my own. "She's absolutely perfect, Ronny."

Ronny kisses the side of my head and I can feel the love and adoration practically radiating off of him. It warms my very core. "You're amazing. I can't believe you did this, baby."

"I didn't do anything special."

Ronny makes a noise of disbelief. "If you truly believe that then I have to step up my game. I want you to always know how special you truly are just from being yourself."

My heart warms and tears prickle behind my eyes. "I love you," I tell him, leaning against his side. His arms are wrapped around me, helping me support our baby. I feel completely encased in love, unable to escape even if I wanted. Which I don't. Now that I'm here, truly loved and safe for the first time, I can't imagine going back to a life where Ronny isn't there.

"Do you have a name?" Star asks after cleaning everything up. Having her here was exactly what I needed. She guided me into trusting my instincts, making this whole process less stressful, less painful, and now, less messy.

"I was thinking of keeping with the J theme," I tell Ronny with a soft smile. "Do you like Jordan?"

Ronny smiles. "I think that's perfect. You are so very perfect, Jordan."

Star and Ronny help me lean back against a pile of pillows. They help me out of my shirt so Jordan and I can enjoy some skin to skin time. I feel at peace.

The only thing that makes this moment better is when Star lets JJ into the RV to meet his new baby sister. Just as we all suspected, he immediately falls in love with her, whispering how he's going to teach her to shift and take her on walks and always look out for her.

When I pictured my future, it was always filled with gritting my teeth and getting through life as best as I could. It was filled with protecting JJ. But now, I'm allowed to live not only for JJ but for me as well. For a long time I was hunting for something, I just didn't realize that thing was Ronny and ultimately, *love*.

EPILOGUE

RONNY

I BURY my toes in the sand. Our little beach vacation had to wait a few days, but we're finally all here. We look like a ridiculous group of tourists, all bunched together on the beach with our giant umbrella that Jeff bought us. Martin refused to put on proper beach attire so he's sitting in his chair with his combat boots, jeans, and black tee. He looks like he could murder someone with that scowl if he tried hard enough.

Hopefully after this tiny break, we'll finally get some sort of proper lead for this case. I know it's really weighing on him, being unable to figure this out. He's always felt like he was all muscle and no brains but we all know that's not true. Once Martin puts his mind to something he *will* figure it out sooner or later.

Cooper on the other hand is laying on a towel in a pair of swimming trunks that are probably one size too small. His skin is turning a pink shade as he reads. I don't miss the way Martin keeps glancing over there but I pretend not to notice.

"Baby time," Zander says, handing Jordan over to me. I take her happily, plopping myself down under the umbrella to keep our baby out of the sun.

"Are you heading into the water with JJ?"

"Yes! He's been itching to get tossed around in the water," Zander says with a wide smile.

"Please be careful. You just had a baby and I don't want you exhausting yourself, okay?"

Zander gets a soft look in his eyes. He ducks down under the umbrella, pulling the brim of my hat so we're face to face. "I love you, you know that, right?"

"I do," I say back, kissing his lips softly. "And I love you, too. Have fun with JJ. I'll miss you."

Zander rolls his eyes. "I'll literally be right over there."

"But that's just so far away. However will I manage without you," I say dramatically, really laying it on thick. He flicks the tip of my hat and runs away giggling. My heart feels near bursting.

"Good lord you two are gross," Carlos murmurs, taking a soda from the cooler and cracking it open. "True mates are also so fucking *sappy*. You're gonna give me cavities if I don't regularly brush when I'm around you guys."

Jeff and Axel just chuckle. "I think someone doth protest too much," Jeff says with a shrug.

Axel sits in the sand with Lily between his legs. She digs in the sand and lets out an adorable giggle. "One of these days it'll be your turn and then you won't be wrinkling your nose."

Carlos sighs. "I don't know if it's in the cards for me, but if Lady Fate deems me fit for such an honor as a true mate, I'm sure you'll be right."

"That wasn't dramatic at all," I murmur, running my fingers through the soft hair at the back of Jordan's head. "You act like you're some villain. You're a great man, Carlos."

"I'll leave that up to Lady Fate," he whispers, standing up and making his way over to Martin.

It's strange. It wasn't that long ago I wouldn't have taken any merit in the idea of Lady Fate. Sure, I'd read about her and knew she was the mother of the supernatural, but I didn't know how hands on she was. Now though? Now I'm a believer. She gave me Zander. She brought me JJ. She truly is guiding her children as best as she can, tying their soul strings together when they're ready.

I know Carlos is a good man and if he has a true mate out there, I know without a doubt that Lady Fate will tie them together at some point.

I look around at my family and smile. We're growing little by little. Part of me wonders if it's smart to keep hunting. We have *children* now. But at the same time I know I can't stop, not while there's still evil out in the world. I want to make this world as positive and *good* as I can for JJ and Jordan and Lily. I want them to feel *safe*.

My eyes dart over to the water, watching as *my mate* tosses our son into the air. He lets out the most beautiful chorus of giggles before he's splashing into the water.

That's my reason for hunting and I'll hold onto that as I

research and find whatever is hunting along the coast. We'll continue our work. We'll continue to hunt. We'll continue to do our best to right some wrongs.

But for today, we rest and marvel at the gifts *and the love* we've been given that makes this life of hunting worth living.

THE END

Want more from the hunters? Keep your eye out for Martin, Cooper, and Dorian's story, **Hunting for Acceptance**, coming soon!

Want more from Toby in the meantime? Check out **A Sucker for You**! This book features an octopus shifter falling for a human, eggpreg, tentacles, and a happily ever after!

If you want to get the latest news from Toby, sign up for **Toby's Newsletter**! He'll keep you informed on new releases, sales, and any exciting news you'll wanna be in the know for.

Plus, you can join **Toby's Patreon** for exclusive content, cover reveals, teasers, and a brand new Patron chosen story!

MORE FROM TOBY WISE

A Collection of Hunters

Between Hunts (Prequel)

Hunting for Redemption

Hunting for Love

A Collection of Strays

Before Fate (Prequel)

Ageless Fate

Touching Fate

Fate's Perfect Timing

Trusting Fate

Submitting to Fate

Bite Sized Fate (Short Story)

Fate's Final Chapter

A Collection of Strays: The Boxset

Studio C

Watching Me

Feral for You

Choosing Me

True For You

ABOUT THE AUTHOR

Toby Wise is a stay at home parent who hails from a tiny town in Wisconsin. Contrary to popular Wisconsin stereotypes, he's not a cheese-head who enjoys beer but rather an introvert who spends all his time on the internet, drinking coffee, spending time with his kid, and cooing about his adorable cat, Pikachu.

In April of 2019, A Collection of Strays was born after the world of fanfiction drew him back into his love of writing. Now he's writing all things omegaverse as long as it includes silly moments and found family.

Facebook Group: Toby's Wiseasses

Toby's Patreon ← Join for exclusive content, early teasers, and ARC's of future books.

Sign up for my Newsletter Here ← Stay up to date on Toby's newest releases.

Toby's Website ← Find all Toby's books, announcements and freebies in one place.

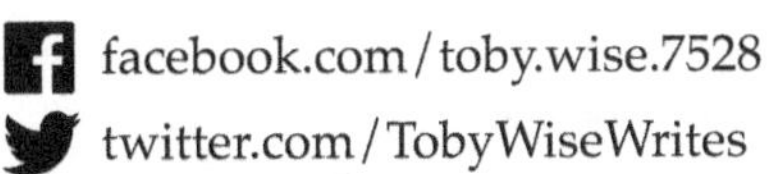

facebook.com / toby.wise.7528

twitter.com / TobyWiseWrites